Dear Romance Reader,

Welcome to a world of breathtaking passion and never-ending romance.

Welcome to *Precious Gem Romances*.

It is our pleasure to present *Precious Gem Romances*, a wonderful new line of romance books by some of America's best-loved authors. Let these thrilling historical and contemporary romances sweep you away to far-off times and places in stories that will dazzle your senses and melt your heart.

Sparkling with joy, laughter, and love, each *Precious Gem Romance* glows with all the passion and excitement you expect from the very best in romance. Offered at a great affordable price, these books are an irresistible value—and an essential addition to your romance collection. Tender love stories you will want to read again and again, *Precious Gem Romances* are books you will treasure forever.

Look for eight fabulous new *Precious Gem Romances* each month—available only at Wal★Mart.

Lynn Brown, Publisher

WINNING ANGEL

Abby Gray

Zebra Books
Kensington Publishing Corp.
http://www.zebrabooks.com

Once upon a time two Gray girls
lived in Tishomingo.
This book is dedicated with love
to the youngest Gray girl . . .
my sister, Patti . . .
who loves happy endings!

ZEBRA BOOKS are published by

Kensington Publishing Corp.
850 Third Avenue
New York, NY 10022

First Printing: August, 1998
10 9 8 7 6 5 4 3 2 1

Printed in the United States of America

One

Clancy Morgan took a second look at the woman standing in the shadows beside the double-wide doors of the banquet hall. There was something about her sexy silhouette that looked familiar, but it had been a long time since he'd seen most of his former classmates, and he couldn't make out her face in the half-light. Perhaps she hadn't been a member of his graduating class, but he just knew that her name was somewhere in the back of his mind.

He suddenly remembered that Angela Conrad used to stand like that, but this woman couldn't be her. The Angela he'd known had always been shy. She'd never show up at a noisy ten-year reunion like this.

"And now, please welcome Dorothy Simpson, the valedictorian of the class of nineteen-thirty-seven," intoned the master of ceremonies from the podium. "Isn't she wonderful?" The crowd applauded as a frail, elderly woman made her way through, and Clancy turned around to pay closer attention to what was going inside the hall.

"Dorothy Simpson is probably the only living member of that class," Janie Sides Walls whispered to him. Clancy smiled and applauded dutifully with the rest of the alumni. But when he looked back to see if the mystery woman was still standing in the shadows, she was gone. Nothing was there but the doors swinging to and fro, as if she had seen enough . . . and left. Clancy wished he had gotten up and gone over, just in case she had been Angela. "Damn," he mumbled under his breath.

Angel was well aware that he had spotted her, felt the questions in his soft brown eyes, and knew beyond a doubt that he hadn't recognized her after all these years. Well, he would. Before the evening was over, Clancy Morgan would know who she was if she had to sit in his lap and tell him herself. But for now she had to get ready. The sound equipment was in place, the microphones set up, the amps ready to bring the house down, and the rest of her band members were in the bus.

"Did you see Clancy?" Bonnie asked when Angel opened the bus door and hopped up on the first step. "Is he here?"

"Yes," Angel said crossly. "Looking just as egotistical and full of himself as ever. And he's even handsomer than he used to be."

"Methinks me hears a note of love gone wrong. Hey, sounds like a good title for our new song. Maybe I just got the inspiration we've needed all these years to take us straight to the top in Nashville," Patty teased.

"Right. Just when we've decided to give up touring," Susan added wryly.

Angel stuck out her tongue at her friends, and peeled faded jean shorts down over her hips. She jerked her knit tank top over her head and slipped on a black silk kimono-style robe, tying the sash tightly around her slim waist.

"Hey, girls, I want to thank you again for tonight. Only real friends would play a two-bit gig like this and I appreciate it. Means a lot to me."

She sat down in front of a built-in vanity, complete with mirror and track lighting, and slapped makeup on her face, covering a fine sprinkling of freckles across her upturned nose. She outlined her big green eyes with a delicate tracing of dark pencil, then brushed mascara on her thick lashes. She flipped her dark brown hair around her face with a styling comb and sat back to look at what she'd created.

Not bad for a backward little girl who'd been scared of her own shadow ten years ago. She wondered if anyone would recognize her. Not that Angel had even planned on attending this reunion any more than the other nine already gone by. But then she had received the letter from the class president and decided—without exactly knowing why—that she'd come to this one. Some of the alumni might doubt she'd even been in their class when they saw her onstage, but after tonight they'd go home and drag out their yearbooks to find her name, and picture. And there she would be in big glasses, which she'd since replaced with contacts, and wildly curly hair, which she still couldn't always tame.

Tonight Angel was going to put away the past, and forget about all those painful years. Tomorrow she was going to wake up a brand-new woman, ready to face whatever life might bring her.

She smiled at her reflection, and peeled the class president's letter off her mirror. It asked for a brief paragraph listing her accomplishments in the decade since she'd finished high school, to be published in the alumni newsletter, and for a contribution of some kind to the reunion. Angel had written back and offered to bring her band and play for the dance—free of charge.

"Better jerk them jeans on, darlin'." Mindy bent down and looked at her in the mirror. "Clancy Morgan's eyes would pop out of his head if you got to gyratin' your hips and the sash of that robe came loose. He'd surely regret being such a jackass all those years ago if he could see what you're hiding under that kimono."

"Oh, hush," Angel laughed. She took her freshly starched white jeans from a hanger and shimmied into them. Then she put on a lace bra and topped it with a sequined vest, flashing red and white horizontal stripes on one side and a ground of blue with white stars on the other. "Lord, all I need is a couple of pasties with tassels," she said, as she checked her appearance in the mirror one last time.

"Hey, we're playing a gig for a bunch of high school alumni. We ain't doing a show for Neddie's Nudie Beauties," Allie pointed out, and pushed open the bus door to lead the way. Their performance was due to start in just ten minutes.

"You five look wonderful," Angel said proudly. Her band members wore identical black jeans and black denim vests with the state flag of Texas embroidered on the backs.

"We clean up pretty good," Susan agreed. "You'd never know we were plain old working women the rest of the week." The band members laughed, and headed for the ballroom.

* * *

"Let's give the equipment one more check before the stampede," Allie said. "Testing." She blew into the first microphone, which produced an ear-squeal, and she nodded toward Bonnie, who was adjusting the amplifiers. "Smoke machine is . . . ready."

Allie turned a knob or two, double-checked the timer, then sat down at her drums and gave a warm-up roll with the sticks. "Ready to rock and roll," she growled into the microphone beside her.

"Ready," Susan breathed into her microphone, and drew her bow across her fiddle, creating a haunting sound which made Angel's blood curdle, just as it did every time they played.

"Then let's knock 'em dead." Mindy stretched her fingers and warmed up on the keyboard with a few bars of Floyd Cramer's "Last Date."

The double-wide doors from the banquet room swung open into the ballroom, and people wandered in, not quite sure this was where they belonged. Clancy Morgan was among them. He and several companions found a table right in front of the small knock-down stage Angel toted around in the equipment trailer behind the bus. Even its slight elevation of twelve inches gave the band an advantage, which was better than being stuck back in a corner of a room on the same level as all the dancers.

"Dark in here," Angel heard a man say. "These itty-bitty candles on the tables don't give much light."

"You didn't complain about that ten years ago at the prom," his wife giggled. "Matter of fact, you wanted to blow the candles out so the ballroom would be darker."

"Yeah, but back then you were fun to be with in the

dark," he teased. The woman pouted. Angel thought she recognized him—wasn't he Jim Moore?

Then the alarm on Allie's watch went off. She did a roll on the drums and pushed a hidden button with her foot. The smoke machine emitted trails of white fog across the stage and a rotating strobe picked up every flicker of candlelight from the tables. When the smoke began to clear, there were five Texas state flags facing the darkened room. Then, from somewhere behind a huge amplifier, Angel stepped out, all aglitter in red, white, and blue sequins.

"Good evening, ladies and gentlemen," she said in a deep, throaty voice. "I'm Angel—and this is the Honky Tonk Band. There's Allie on the drums." She stood aside and Allie stood up, all five feet ten inches of her, to bow and give the audience fifteen seconds of a percussion riff.

"And Patty on rhythm guitar." One of the flags turned around to reveal a blond woman, even taller than the drummer and built like an athlete. Patty bowed, and struck a chord and waved to the people, hoping for an enthusiastic crowd. Lord, but she hated to play to a dead bunch and these alimni sure didn't look as lively as the folks they'd played to last night.

"Bonnie, on steel." The second flag turned, and Bonnie made the guitar slung around her neck whine like a baby. "Susan, on the fiddle." Angel waved to her left, and a short woman with red hair perched a fiddle on her shoulder and let them hear a tantalizing bit of a classic country tune.

"And over here is Mindy on the keyboard." The final flag turned slowly to face the alumni of Tishomingo High School. "Hi, ya'll," she said huskily into the mike as Mindy made the keyboard do everything but sing.

"And this is Angel!" The president of the alumni association hopped up on the stage at the right moment to introduce her. "You might remember her as Angela Conrad, and she and these gorgeous band members have agreed to play for us tonight for free. Let's make them welcome and get ready for a show. These ladies will be at the Arbuckle Ballroom in Davis next Friday night for their final gig, so we're lucky to get 'em. Angel says she's tired of working all week and the weekends, too. So give them a big hand to let them know how much we appreciate them playing for us." He started the applause and the audience followed suit as he hopped back down off the stage and took his wife's hand, leading her to the middle of the dance floor and waiting for the first song to begin.

"Wind 'em up, girls," Angel whispered and grabbed a mike and started off the evening with a surefire crowd pleaser. Mindy tinkled the keyboard keys and Allie kept a steady beat with the brushes on the drums. Angel strutted across the stage, sequins flashing in the strobe lights, and the long diamond drops that dangled from her ears glittering in her dark-brown shoulder-length curls.

Before long, there were at least twenty couples in the middle of the floor, dancing in one way or another. Several were doing something between the twist and the jerk and an older couple were executing a pretty fine jitterbug, and Angel made them all feel like she was singing just to them. But she kept looking down at the table where Clancy Morgan sat alone while his friends tried to keep up with the beat on the dance floor. Evidently Melissa—if he had married her—

couldn't accompany him tonight. Or maybe he hadn't married her. Now wouldn't that be a hoot?

She put her left hand on her hip and struck that familiar pose, and memories from that summer ten years ago flooded Clancy's mind. What had happened to the Angela Conrad he'd known? She was supposed to marry old Billy Joe Summers and raise a shack full of snotty-nosed kids. She was supposed to work in a sewing factory, supporting Billy Joe's life-threatening drinking habit. She wasn't supposed to be on a stage, belting out songs by famous artists.

Patty started a strong rhythm and Angel stepped off the stage and mixed with the people in the dancing crowd, singing into a cordless mike. Then she sat down on the table right in front of Clancy, wiggled her shoulders and sang to him as she looked right in his eyes, realizing that he had indeed finally recognized her. There was a haunted, lost look in his eyes, as if he wanted to say something, but he just sat there without saying a word, shaking his head in disbelief.

She looked something like the old Angela, except she wasn't wearing glasses. She leaned toward him far enough that he could see down the front of her vest, and a red heat stirred inside him as he remembered how soft her skin was there. She sang while the girls provided back-up on the stage, then suddenly she wiggled and before he could blink she was back on the stage.

"Hey, Mike Griffin, pull that woman up a little closer. You sure danced closer than that when we were in high school," Angel teased in the middle of another song, a more romantic one, while the band played the break.

She glanced at the table to her left, and saw that

Clancy still had a bewildered look on his face, as if his eyes couldn't believe his ears. It was a heady feeling, knowing him well enough to know what was in his heart. Angel could still list his every accomplishment. Quarterback from tenth through twelfth grade, taking the team to the state championship all three years. Debate champion, too, winning the regional trophy during his senior year.

But Angel would bet dollars to donuts that if Clancy had to hop up on the stage right now and speak, he'd be as awkward as he'd been that summer night after their graduation. He couldn't hide his feelings then and he obviously still hadn't learned how. Because his long face told her he was having a hard time dealing with her putting on a show for the alumni organization. In fact, his ego appeared to be *severely* deflated.

"We'll have a fifteen-minute break while we grab something to drink." Allie pulled her microphone close to her face. "See y'all in a quarter of an hour."

Before Clancy could make sense of his thoughts, Angel had gone out the side door, surrounded by her band. He stretched out his long limbs, amazed that he'd sat still for an hour and a half while memories and her presence tormented him. He smiled and nodded at several of his old friends as he made his way to the doors leading out to the balcony, where he could see the bus parked in the lot behind the ballroom. It was black with gold metallic lettering, that sparkled in the light from the streetlamps. The word "Angel" had a crooked halo slung over the capital "A," and "The Honky Tonk Band" had little gold devils with pitchforks sitting on each of the "o" letters.

He remembered the nights when she'd sung along with the radio in his new red Camaro, and he hadn't been able to tell which was the real singer and which was Angela. Who would have ever thought she'd be running around in her own bus with a band of women who looked like candidates for the Dallas Cowboy Cheerleaders?

When he'd sent in the questionnaire saying he would attend the reunion, he hadn't even thought about Angela showing up. She was almost the one voted most likely *not* to succeed. Although hardly a day had gone by in the past ten years that something didn't make him think of Angela Conrad, but he'd long since learned to disassociate himself from what had really happened that summer. It was as if it happened to someone in a book and he'd just read about it. He hadn't really sat on the creek bank with her late into the nights and let the minnows nibble their toes. He hadn't actually walked away that last night, knowing she was crying. No, it couldn't have been him. It was someone else in a novel, or a movie and he just remembered the details too well.

"Whew." Allie dabbed her face with a tissue. "Pretty lively crowd for a bunch of has-beens."

"Hey," Angel giggled nervously. "They're mostly my age. I belong to that crowd."

"Yeah, like I belong at the pearly gates of heaven," Susan laughed, her blue eyes twinkling. "You outgrew them years ago. Don't let these hicks make you think you still belong to their world."

"Thanks." Angel pretended to slap her cheek. "I needed that."

"Well, I can see why you were so stuck on that Clancy. He fills out them Wranglers pretty damned good," Patty sighed. "And those big, wide shoulders about gave me the vapors." She fluttered her long eyelashes. "Maybe you oughta give him another chance, Angel. Lord, handsome as he is, I'd give him a chance if he wasn't already wearin' your brand."

"Hell," Angel snorted. "He never wore my brand. He's free for the taking if you're interested. Least I think he isn't married. But stand assured, he's about as trustworthy as those two little devils painted on the side of this bus."

"No, thanks," Patty said, putting on fresh lipstick. "You can keep him. Then tame him or kill him but don't give him to me."

"Me neither," Mindy giggled and pushed the bus door open. She gulped in the hot night air, and looked up at the starlit sky to see if there might be a stray cloud with a few raindrops to spare. "Hey, look up on the balcony when you come outside, Angel. Clancy's up there staring down here like he can't believe his little eyeballs."

"Yeah? That's nothing new. He always did look down on me." Angel was suddenly tired. Her bones ached like they'd never ached before during a performance . . . and so did her stupid heart. "Another hour and a half and we'll take this bus home and park it. Then I'll forget about Clancy Morgan and get on with life."

"Sure," Bonnie said, "You'll forget Clancy when you're stone-cold dead and planted six feet down. Women don't forget first loves, and they *never* forget a first love who did them dirty."

Two

Angel flipped the light switch just inside the massive doors of her office and slipped off her shoes. She padded across the thick ivory carpet and plopped down in an oversize blue velvet chair behind an antique French provincial desk. She tossed the alumni newsletter on the desk, laced her hands behind her head and tried to calm down.

She hadn't meant for Clancy to affect her this way. She'd gone there to give her former classmates their comeuppance. She'd planned to leave with a smile on her face and never think about any of them ever again. Several former acquaintances had made a point of stopping by the stage between songs and saying hello to her, but Clancy left just after the last song without a word. But then, what could he say? He'd made his choice ten years ago and it hadn't left any room for a change of heart.

Angel noticed Patty's car, the last to leave the garage on the bottom floor of the company, drive down the street. The other girls had already disappeared in their own vehicles into the early-morning darkness. Next Friday they would be playing the Arbuckle Ballroom in Davis, Oklahoma, and then a new band called The Gamblers would pick up the bus and have it repainted with their logo. It was high time for the Honky Tonk Band to go out with a flourish and retire. The girls enjoyed performing, but they needed their weekends these days. Allie was married and her husband Tyler complained that he never saw her on weekends. Susan lived with her boyfriend Richie, and they needed more quality time together. Bonnie was engaged and planning an October wedding, and Mindy was in the middle of a divorce. Besides, none of them were getting any younger. Angel sighed, thinking about how she could catch up on all the work at the farm when she stopped touring. And she had this oil business to run as well.

She thought about Tishomingo again. Main Street had changed a little in the past ten years. The courthouse was new and the cafe had a different name these days, and there was a new pharmacy standing where the Nazarene church used to be. There was only one grocery store instead of two, but Chuck's Grocery, where her granny used to buy the best jalapeño cheese in the whole world, was still doing business. She'd looked up Pennington Creek when they'd crossed the bridge over it into town, and noticed that it hadn't changed at all. The same trees still shaded the sandbar below the dam, and the memories of what had happened night after night on a blanket in the privacy of those trees were so real she could almost smell Clancy's aftershave again.

Angel picked up the newsletter and began to read. Each page had a classmate's name at the top and a brief summary of their accomplishments in the past ten years. Apparently almost everyone had sent in the questionnaire whether or not they had attended the alumni banquet and the dance. She found her own bio and reread it. *Because of previous engagements, I'm not able to attend the banquet. However, my band and I—*

Angel and the Honky Tonk Band—will play for the dance free of charge if you would like. Let me know at the following address. Angela Conrad. She'd added a box number in Denison, Texas. But no one knew that she had rented the box for one month just for the return answer to her letter.

She found Clancy's reply. Since leaving high school, he'd graduated from the University of Oklahoma with a bachelor's degree in geology and chemistry and a minor in education. Then he'd enlisted in the Air Force, and had been stationed in Virginia for most of his four-year career, and had gone to graduate school for a master's in education. Just recently he'd come back to Oklahoma and started teaching in an Oklahoma City high school. Under *Marital Status,* he had marked an X beside *Divorced.*

So he probably had married Melissa after all. But what had happened? By small town society's rules, Mr. and Mrs. Clancy Morgan were supposed to be living happily ever after. Suddenly Angel wished she had subscribed to the Tishomingo weekly newspaper. Then at least she would have known who'd married whom, who had children, and so forth. She knew very little about her former classmates.

When her granny had driven their old green pickup truck out of Tishomingo that long-ago fall day, Angel hadn't even looked back in the rearview mirror for one last glimpse of the place where she'd lived since she was three years old. She hadn't left anything behind but heartaches and she didn't need to look back at the fading lights of town to recapture them. They would be with her forever.

She looked through the newsletter to see what Billy Joe Summers was doing these days. She hadn't seen him at the dance even though she'd scanned the ball-room several times to see if there was a six-foot, five-inch gangly man standing shyly on the sidelines. Billy Joe had always been nice to her and that awful night on the sandbar when she'd sat with her feet in the warm water, it had been Billy Joe's name that Clancy had mentioned so scornfully.

"Hello again, Mr. Henry." Angel picked up a worn teddy bear sitting on top of her filing cabinet, and held him, just for old times' sakes. Mr. Henry had listened sympathetically to all her tales of woe in the years since she'd been given him for her fifth birthday . . . and here she was, still feeling sorry for herself.

She wondered how her memories of Tishomingo could still be so vivid. After all, she hadn't ever wanted to go back, even though she and her granny had lived there for fifteen years, since the day she'd turned three years old. Angel had spent her babyhood in nearby Kemp, and although they visited her great-grandpa at the farm there a couple of times a year, she couldn't recollect anything about it.

When Angel had turned eighteen, her great-grandpa Poppa John had died, and left his twenty acres to his only child—Angel's grandmother. After his estate had been settled, she and her granny had left Tishomingo and gone back to Kemp. And it hadn't happened a minute too soon, in anyone's opinion. Angel remembered the day all too well . . .

"Don't stay out late, Angela. We've got to pack in the morning," her granny reminded her. "Got to be out of the house before midnight or pay more rent, you know."

"I know." Angela went out the front door and

walked west toward the dam. All summer she'd gone swimming every evening in Pennington Creek, and it was a good thing August had arrived, because her bikini was beginning to look as worn-out as her jeans. Most times it seemed like just a hop, skip, and jump from her house to the swimming hole, but that evening the walk took forever.

Angel shimmied out of her shorts and shirt and sat in her bikini on the sandbar, soaking her feet in the lukewarm water while she waited. Clancy wouldn't be there for another half-hour so she could think about what she had to say. She'd known the first time they'd accidentally met each other in this very place that she was flirting with big trouble, but she'd been in love with Clancy Morgan since kindergarten. If he would just touch her hand or kiss her one time before she moved away, she could survive forever on the memories.

Clancy plopped down on the sandbar. "I've got something to tell you, Angela."

"I've got something to tell you, Clancy." She sat up and drew her knees to her chin and wrapped her arms around her legs.

And when she told him, he said, "Why don't you just marry Billy Joe? He's been in love with you since the first grade."

"Go to hell, Clancy," she found enough courage to say. "I don't need you anyway. I can take care of myself. Just leave me alone."

Without another word, Clancy turned and walked up the bank to his pretty red car. She watched the car back up to the dirt road, then turn left to cross the bridge, and when it was out of sight, Angela buried her face in her hands and sobbed, heartbroken and alone . . .

* * *

Angel sighed deeply and pulled her thoughts back to the present. She turned to the newsletter page with Billy Joe's bio. He was living in San Francisco where he was working as a computer technician. Under *Comments* he had written: *I want to tell Angela Conrad hello wherever she is. She was the only person who treated me like an equal, and I have often thought of her. She was the one who told me to stop drinking years ago and got me on the road to recovery. Since then, I have come out of the closet and have a wonderful companion, Stephen. We are both very active in the gay rights movement and have had articles published in several papers and magazines.*

Her amused response started as a weak giggle, grew into a chuckle, and then a full-fledged roar. So Billy Joe was gay. Now wasn't that just the frosting on the cake tonight? She hoped Clancy Morgan had read Billy Joe's contribution to the alumni newsletter. Perhaps it would help him remember his asinine remark to her that long-ago night beside Pennington Creek.

Clancy let himself into the house where he had grown up. His father had died while he was in Virginia with the Air Force and now his mother lived there alone. She was sleeping already and he tiptoed to the dining room where he turned on the light above the table and set his newsletter down. He brewed a pot of strong coffee, since he had a feeling he wasn't going to sleep much tonight anyway.

He poured himself a mug of black coffee, sat down at the table, and turned to Angela Conrad's brief bio. His heart fluttered softly, then dropped to a dull ache when he read what she'd written. He still didn't know anything, except that she probably lived in Denison, since she gave a box number there. She'd given no personal information and Clancy wondered if she was married, single, or divorced. She didn't mention it if she had a child or children, and she was still using her maiden name.

Clancy burned his lip on the hot coffee and swore softly. "Damn it all," he muttered, but he was angry with more than the coffee. He was mad at himself all over again as he remembered that hot August night when he'd gone to see her to break it off . . .

His girlfriend Melissa had begun to suspect there was someone else in his life, and she would have a first-rate hissy fit if she found out he was sneaking around with Angela Conrad every night after he left *her.*

Angela had been waiting for him in her usual place, with her feet in the water, wearing only a bikini. Her jean shorts and that orange T-shirt that was too big for her were tossed up on the creek bank. Her brown curls were pulled back into a ponytail and she looked like a little girl. But then she was only five feet three inches tall and barely weighed a hundred and ten pounds.

He remembered telling her to marry Billy Joe Summers and her telling him to go to hell. And he'd never seen her again, from that night until now . . .

Clancy and Melissa had gone to Oklahoma University, just as they'd planned since their sophomore year. At the end of the first semester, he had casually asked a former classmate about Billy Joe and Angela and learned that both of them had left Tishomingo at about the same time, and that was all anyone knew. He'd heaved a sigh of relief.

He and Melissa had married right after their college graduation and she'd taught school while he was in the Air Force. Until the year she'd come home and told Clancy she wanted out. She'd fallen in love with the principal of her school and they were planning to marry as soon as the divorce was final. That had ended what he'd thought would be a military career. Clancy had come back to Oklahoma then, and landed his present job teaching chemistry at an Oklahoma City high school.

He turned the pages until he found Billy Joe Summers' name. Maybe Billy Joe lived in Denison, too . . . and maybe he'd married Angela after all, and they had had that pack of kids and she and her band played border town dives just to pay the bills.

But when Clancy read Billy Joe's page, he felt just plain foolish. So Billy Joe was gay . . . and Angela sure hadn't looked poor. Two-bit bands that played for border town dives didn't have customized buses, and none of them had smoke machines and their own knockdown stages, and none of them played at the Arbuckle Ballroom, either. Angela and her band had done well, but evidently hadn't hit the big time, either. And now her name was Angel . . .

He'd called her that sometimes, he realized.

So just what in the hell was she up to? *None of your damn business,* his conscience told him. *You gave up any rights to know what she was doing with her life that August night down by the creek when you were eighteen years old.*

He turned out the light and went to the living room where he leaned back in his father's recliner and thought about Angela Conrad. His angel—once upon a time.

Angel turned off her office lights and pulled the door shut. She carried a burgundy leather briefcase in one hand and her laptop in the other. She pushed the button for the elevator to take her down to the ground-floor garage where her black Jaguar was parked. It was time to go home. The two-story Conrad Oil Enterprises, Inc., building disappeared in her rearview mirror as she drove to Main Street in Denison and then east on a farm road.

She thought about the first days when she and the girls had formed the band and played the border town dives in Cartwright, Colbert, Yuba, and Willis. They didn't even have a name then, just a few instruments and a need to make a couple of dollars on the weekends to keep them in college. That was before Conrad Oil Enterprises had been even a glimmer of an idea.

One night they'd unloaded their equipment at the Dixie Pixie club in Yuba while an old man wearing faded overalls watched. He swilled his liquor from a Mason jar and said to his wife, a big woman in red stretch pants, "Well, looky here, Momma. There's a pretty little angel with her honky tonk band. Guess we died and went to heaven."

The old man had named their band right then and Angel wondered if he was even around anymore to know how far she and the Honky Tonk Band had come in the past years.

She crossed the river bridge and turned left into Hendrix, Oklahoma, then drove several miles more to her farm. It was only twenty acres, but it was home, and home was where her heart was this morning.

The sun was an orange ball on the horizon when she pulled the car into the oval driveway. When she opened the door, she could smell the welcoming fragrance of roses. Jimmy's gardening skills kept the rosebushes in the pink, even if the Oklahoma winds and hot, blistering sun tried to rob him of the blooms at this time of year. But as she'd told him so many times, his thumbs were greener than spring grass, and he could make silk plants reproduce if he wanted to. The house was dark, but then she hadn't expected Hilda to be there yet. The housekeeper, Hilda, didn't usually arrive until midmorning and then she left in the middle of the afternoon, unless Angel was there and needed her longer.

She opened the gate to the white picket fence surrounding the two-story farmhouse which looked like it had been there since the turn of the century. But she'd had the house custom-built just four years before. It was her dream house, and Angel loved everything about it.

She crossed the verandah which wrapped the house on three sides and noticed that the blue morning glories climbing the porch posts were starting to open with the approach of dawn. She unlocked the front door.

She always liked to arrive early in the morning and have a few hours by herself. This morning in particular she needed the tranquillity more than she'd needed it in years.

Angel boiled a kettle of water and poured it over green tea leaves in a ceramic pot and waited for the tea to steep. She propped up her feet on the hassock beside the cold fireplace and watched the sun come up through the French doors leading out onto the patio. As it topped the well house, she could see the silhouette of her first oil well, now standing as a silent sentinel to all that was hers, and the beginning of the successful enterprise known as Conrad Oil, which had grown so fast it still didn't seem quite real.

Dawn was gone and a new Sunday was born before she poured the lukewarm tea in a cup and put a slice of Hilda's home-made bread in the toaster. Granny would have liked this house. She would have fussed about the cost of it, but she would have grinned that big smile which made her eyes disappear in a face so full of wrinkles it looked like a road map, and she would have liked the peacefulness of a new home. Though Granny never would have put up with someone else cleaning her house and baking her bread. She would turn over in her grave if she knew Angel paid a gardener these days to keep the roses blooming and the morning glories watered, but then when Granny had inherited the property from her father and moved with Angel to the original three-room house on this twenty acres, she hadn't owned an oil company.

Angel buttered the bread with sweet butter. Someday she might have to watch fat grams and calories, but not today. She liked real butter on her toast, just as her granny had. Thoughts of the past flitted through her mind.

She and her grandmother had arrived with all their belongings in the back of that old rusty green truck which looked like an accident waiting for a place to happen. The old house had only three rooms—a small living room and kitchen and one bedroom where she and Granny put their twin beds, and a tiny bathroom just off the living room. They'd lived there happily enough until four years later, when her granny had died peacefully in her sleep.

The preacher had read a poem and the Twenty-third Psalm at the graveside service, and a few church members showed up along with the five girls in her band. Three months later, Angel had mortgaged the property and drilled a gusher. From there, she'd taken one giant step after another, until today she was the major stockholder and president of her own oil company, based in Denison, with branch offices in Oklahoma and Louisiana as well.

Angel closed her eyes. She had all the money she could spend in a lifetime . . . all the excitement of unexpected success . . . all the peacefulness of a country home to enjoy for the rest of her life . . . but none of it would ever ease the cold, blue loneliness in her heart.

Three

Next Friday night, Clancy parked his Ford Bronco a comfortable distance away from the big black bus sitting in the crowded parking lot of the Arbuckle Ballroom, just off I-35 west of Davis. He could hear the *thump, thump, thump* of the music every time the doors opened and someone either went in or came back out. It was well past midnight and he'd been sitting there for over an hour.

He wanted to pay the cover charge and go inside to

listen to Angel sing, to watch her move with that sexy confidence she hadn't had in high school, to breathe in the essence of her that sent his senses reeling, but he didn't want her to know he was there. He had thought at first that he would simply wait beside the bus and try to talk to her when she finished the gig.

Whether she liked it or not, he was going to find out what really happened after he went away to college. It occurred to him that he didn't deserve to know after the way he'd treated her, but perhaps she'd forgiven him. They were adults, now, after all, and he had a feeling that his mind wouldn't be eased until he knew the whole story.

Clancy realized the music had died down. The doors opened, but it wasn't the band members who came out. A big man dressed in black jeans and cowboy boots with silver tips on the pointed toes stumbled out with his arm around a skinny, hard-looking blonde wearing a denim miniskirt and red cowboy boots. Then another couple staggered forth, giggling as they held each other up long enough to get the car door open and drive away. Angel finally came out with her band members and started loading equipment. The lady she'd introduced as Patty, the rhythm guitar player, sat down in the driver's seat and revved up the motor.

The bus pulled into the parking lot of an all-night convenience store across the highway from the Ballroom. Patty went inside and came out carrying a big bag of chips and a brown bag full of what he supposed was junk food. As he followed the bus, she made a sharp right at the overpass bridge and headed south on the interstate.

Traffic was sparse at that time of night so Clancy lingered a quarter of a mile behind them. They crossed the Red River into Texas, going west at Gaines-ville. The bus made a quick stop, in Whitesboro and one of the girls got out. Allie, the drummer, waved at the black bus and hopped into a new model red mini-van and drove north. Then the bus headed west until it arrived in Sherman, and turned north to Denison. He managed to keep the taillights in view as it stopped and started through town, finally going down an alley and disappearing through huge garage doors in the bottom floor of an enormous building.

He eased into a parking place reserved for banking customers only in the lot across the alley and studied the sign which was lit up with overhead bulbs. "Conrad Oil Enterprises?" he said out loud. "Holy cow. Angel must have a rich uncle." He wondered why she had never mentioned anyone in her family having money . . . at least not to him.

The doors opened again and four vehicles drove out of the building's garage. The first one was a dark Lincoln with the window rolled down, driven by Bon-nie, the steel guitar player. A red Cadillac followed her, and Susan, the girl who'd played the fiddle, waved to the car behind her as she pulled out onto the road and went south. The third car was a black convertible with Mindy behind the wheel. The last one was a white pickup, and although Clancy could tell there was only one person in the truck, he didn't know if it was Patty or Angel. Just as he turned the key to start up the engine, he caught a glimpse of Angel, still wearing her sequined vest, standing beside the bus and watching the doors of the garage close.

Clancy slid down in the seat and waited an hour. Finally, just after dawn, a black Jaguar rolled out of the garage and turned north. He followed it out of the alley, down the side street, and onto Main Street where she turned right and almost lost him. Angel drove faster than the speed limit and crossed the railroad tracks as if they weren't even there. When he hit the tracks, he bounced around like a puppet inside a rainbarrel, but he managed to hold onto the wheel and keep the back end of her car in sight. The road they were traveling on had to have more dog legs in it than the city pound, he thought crossly. It twisted this way and that, and she never seemed to even tap the brakes.

Then Angel's car made an abrupt left turn. He thought she glanced up in the rearview mirror and spotted him, but evidently she hadn't, because she squealed the tires and took off across a rusty old one-lane bridge, with him right behind her. When he reached the middle of the bridge and looked down, his heart did a flip-flop. Clancy had always been afraid of heights, and this bridge had to be at least a mile above the Red River that flowed below, marking the border between Texas and Oklahoma.

Surely Angel could have gone home via the interstate, Clancy thought. Anything higher than a two-foot stepladder made him nervous. He shuddered again, but didn't look down at the muddy water. Why in the devil would she want to drive over a deathtrap like this?

Then the Jaguar took another sharp turn and sped down the road past a cafe on one side and a beer hall on the other. Then suddenly it stopped in front of him so fast, he almost slammed into the rear bumper. Before he could collect his wits she had the door jerked open and was standing with her left hand on her hip, an angry look in her eye and a pistol in her right hand pointed right at his nose.

"Why in the hell are you following me?" she demanded, then realized who was behind the wheel. "Clancy? What in the hell are *you* following me for?"

"Well . . . I . . . I . . . just . . ." he stammered. "Put that damn gun down, Angel. I'm not here to hurt you."

She lowered the weapon. "Just why the hell are you here?"

"I just wanted to know where you lived. No one knew," he said honestly.

"Oh."

"Got a problem here, Miss Conrad?" A middle-aged policeman opened the door of the cafe.

"Nope. I thought I did, but it turns out I know this man," she told him.

"Sure?" the policeman asked cautiously as he noticed the gun still in her hand.

"Yes, I'm sure," she said. "He's an old classmate of mine. I'm fine, Bruce. Thanks for checking on me."

"Okay. I know you have a permit for that gun. But be careful who you point it at. If he really is an old classmate, I don't know why you have it out of your purse," the officer said as he got into his black and white patrol car.

Clancy and Angel watched him drive away, and then Clancy spoke.

"I want some answers," he demanded.

"Oh? I wanted some answers ten years ago, Clancy. But you only gave me some unsolicited advice about marrying Billy Joe. So what gives you the right to expect answers now?" Her eyes flashed and her hands shook so badly, she nearly dropped her pearl-handled .22 pistol. Angel couldn't decide whether she wanted to kill him . . . or kiss him. And his reply didn't help her make up her mind.

"Maybe I don't have any right to talk to you at all.

I'll leave you alone if that's what you want. I just wanted
to satisfy my curiosity, I guess. I waited in the parking
lot at that ballroom up in Davis and followed you. Do
you work for that oil company or something?"

"It's none of your damned business where I work
or what I do. Go home to your small town, Clancy. I'm
not a naive little girl anymore. And I'm sure as hell
not impressed with you." Angel slammed the door to
his Bronco and stomped back to her car.

She whipped the Jaguar back out onto the highway,
spinning up the gravel. He watched the taillights getting smaller and smaller, and then, on the spur of the
moment and against his better judgment, he followed
her.

Clancy noticed a sign that said Muddy Creek Road
when they turned right and suddenly his tires were
crunching over gravel, but she didn't slow down
much. Just when he thought it was as bad as it could
get, the road turned into little more than a pathway
with tall weeds towering over his vehicle. He'd need
a machete to chop his way out of this mess if he ever
ran out of gas. Grass grew at least knee-high in the
middle of the two ruts, and he wondered if she was
aware of him behind her and was leading him out into
the middle of someone's farm pond to drown him.
Then she whipped the Jaguar to the right and down
a beautiful macadam lane with trees and flowers grow-
ing on both sides.

Angel didn't stop to smell the roses or enjoy the
morning glories as she stomped across the wooden
porch to the front door of the farmhouse. She had
the door opened and was about to flip the light switch
when she heard the scrunch of gravel as Clancy drove
up. *Great.* All she wanted was a few hours to herself,
and he had the nerve to follow her. Her nerves were

exposed and raw after actually facing him and hearing him call her name.

She heard his car door slam and turned to see Clancy walking up the flower-edged sidewalk to the porch. Her first thought was to pull that little revolver out of her purse and shoot him before he reached her porch; her second was to meet him halfway and drag him up to her bedroom.

"This where you live?" he asked casually. Leave it to Clancy to act as if nothing important had ever happened between them.

"No, this is where my boyfriend and I live together," she retorted as hatefully as she could, and then wondered where that lie came from.

"Oh, really?" He was beside her. "What's his name?"

"Nosey, aren't you?" she said.

"You still haven't told me the story of your life," he said calmly. Clancy sat down in the porch swing as if he owned the place.

"I'm going to bed. I played a gig half the night, and I plan to work here all weekend. Looks like you've been up all night, too, but that's your problem, Clancy. Good night or morning or whatever. Most important, good-bye!" she said, and shut the door.

Angel bypassed the kitchen and went straight upstairs, took a quick shower and crawled into the four-poster bed. So now he knew where she lived and where she worked and he would probably be back. But even if he came back a million times she wouldn't tell him anything. What had happened after he'd left her ten years ago simply was none of his business. She pulled a pillow over her eyes and willed her tired mind and body to go to sleep.

She awoke in the middle of the afternoon. She

could hear a lawn mower in the backyard, so evidently Jimmy was working back there. The noise of the vacuum cleaner in the living room let her know Hilda was busy.

Which reminded Angel to get busy herself. For one thing, it had been at least a month since she's been over to the cemetery and she knew the weeds were probably knee deep. She had planted a flower garden on and around the grave sites this past spring. On a whim, she'd then put a white wrought-iron bench at the end of the graves so she could sit and think. What might her granny have told her to do about a problem like this?

A problem named Clancy.

The man was back and he wasn't going to leave her alone, no matter what he said. She snuggled down in her bed and remembered again the look on his face when she'd told him she was pregnant that night on the sandbar by Pennington Creek. Every word he'd said still rang in her ears . . .

"Angela, you mean to say you aren't on the pill? Hellfire and damnation, I never would've—" Clancy stopped and glared at her. "Well, it won't work. I'm not going to marry you. Lord, I'd be the laughingstock of the whole damn town of Tishomingo."

"Did I ask you to marry me?" She looked up at him. "I sure wouldn't want to upset your precious plans with your sweet little Melissa, now would I? Heaven help us if *she* didn't get her way."

"Don't you talk about her like that! She's got more class than—"

Angela stood up and slapped him soundly across

the cheek. "Go back to her then. And forget all about us. About everything we did this summer. Go ahead and marry Melissa," she said in a voice just barely above a whisper, hoarse with emotion.

"Don't you dare go to my folks and tell them." Clancy held his red cheek. His eyes flashed anger and the deep cleft in his chin quivered just slightly. He raked his hand through his dark-brown hair, not knowing whether to walk away or sit down and talk some more.

"I'll tell whoever I want." Angela turned her back on him.

"I've got five hundred dollars of my graduation money left. I'll give it to you for an abortion," he offered.

"Just go away, Clancy. I don't know why I ever thought I loved you, anyway. It's a cinch you never did love me." She stepped out of the water and grabbed her shorts.

"Sit down," Clancy said. "Listen to me. There's a solution. Bob got Janie in the family way last year and they told everyone they were going to the mall in Oklahoma City and to the movies, and then he was taking her to her girlfriend's for the night. They got a motel room and stayed in it after the abortion. Nothing bad happened."

Angela buttoned her shorts and sat down beside him. She put her feet in the water and watched the tiny fish nibble on her polished red toenails. "I didn't do this on purpose," she declared.

"Don't worry about it," he sighed. "My checkbook is in the car." He nodded toward the Camaro his parents had given him for graduation. "I suppose you can get someone to take you."

"Forget it."

"What are you going to do?" he asked. "Don't you dare tell everyone in town it's mine. Maybe you could marry Billy Joe Summers. You know he's been in love with you since we were little kids," he said sarcastically.

"I'm going home."

Angela stood up. "I haven't really been in love with you, Clancy. I was in love with the boy I thought you were. Don't worry about this baby. Don't let the thought of it ever cross your mind again. It's not yours . . . it's mine, and I'll take care of it. Just go on home."

"Oh, hell, Angela, use your brain. You're smart even if you are—"

"What?" She scowled at him. "Poor? Well, that didn't stop you from kissing me and making love with me all summer, did it? I've been a complete fool about you, Clancy. Someday you're going to look back and think about tonight, though. And I hope your heart hurts when you do. I hope it aches just like mine is aching right now. But between now and then, don't ever think about this baby we made again." Angela walked away from him without looking back.

"Don't worry, honey," Granny had told her that night when she'd gone home crying. "He's a rich kid and he's not about to do right by you. He'll marry that stuck-up girl he's been seein' all this time, and we'll take care of ourselves. We'll be movin' tomorrow just like we planned, and you're goin' to college this fall on that grant money you got. Things look tough tonight, but it'll work out, Angela. Stop your weepin' and learn your lessons."

"But I love him, Granny," she sobbed.

"I hope you do," she snorted. "Be a terrible thing

if you didn't. But cryin' ain't goin' to make anything different. We'll manage and nobody will ever know," she said. . . .

Angel shook her head, clearing the memories and threw back the covers. She crawled out of bed, threw the covers over the pillows and picked out an old pair of jeans from the closet. She wiggled down into them and jerked a T-shirt over her head. She pulled her curls up into a ponytail, put on a pair of sneakers and was ready.

"Got a guest," Hilda said when she reached the kitchen. The housekeeper smiled in an odd way, and Angel wondered what had happened while she'd been sleeping.

"Where?" Angel asked.

"Out there on the swing. Asleep. Lot of man to be curled up like that. I told him to get out of here when I come in to work, but he said you knew he was there and he wasn't leavin' until you talked to him. So I just ignored him. He's been asleep about two hours. Just sat there swinging all mornin'. Is he all there? You know, is he a little bit strange or something?" Hilda's wise old eyes narrowed slightly.

"He's strange all right," Angel had to smile. Clancy could sleep until he grew gray hair and died in that swing. She'd even see to it his sorry carcass was taken home to his mother and they could bury him—still in the swing—but she wasn't talking to him . . . not ever again.

"I'm going to the cemetery today to take care of the plots."

Angel slapped a sandwich together and put it in a paper sack along with an apple and a can of Coke.

"But I'm leaving by the back way. If Clancy wakes up, tell him I've gone to Europe for a month."

"Oh, Angel, are you takin' a vacation? Honey, you've needed one for a long time." Hilda patted her on the back.

"Hell, no!" Angel giggled. "But don't tell Clancy that. He doesn't need to know where I am."

"Oh," Hilda said. "So that's Clancy Morgan out there, is it?"

"Hilda, don't you dare tell him anything," Angel pointed her finger and shook her head.

"Me? I wouldn't give that man the sweat from my brow if he was dyin' of thirst. Not me!" Hilda fumed as she picked up her broom and started toward the fireplace to sweep the flagstone in front of it.

"See you later," Angel whispered, and eased out the back door.

Hilda counted to ten slowly, then went out to the front porch where Clancy was snoring loudly on the porch swing. So this was the sorry bastard who'd caused her Angel to be single at the age of twenty-eight . . . who'd made her cry when she was younger, and who'd upset her today. He wasn't a bad-looking fellow—tall, well built, dark hair, dark stubble starting to show on his face where he needed to shave.

She hooked the broom handle in the back of the swing and shoved with all her might. One minute Clancy was dreaming of the sweet angel he used to know in his arms beside the creek bank, and the next he was flying across the porch, grabbing at the air for something to hold on to. Then his eyes sprang open just in time to see the wood floor as he landed face-down.

"Why did you do that?" he sputtered as he sat up.

"Me?" Hilda looked shocked.

The old green pickup he remembered from high school roared around the end of the house and out onto the dirt road headed west. "Where's she going?" He sat up, checking his nose to see if it was bleeding.

"I wouldn't know, you dirty scoundrel. But she drives fast. Perhaps you'd best haul your butt on out to that fancy car of yours and get out of here."

"Kept my promise," Hilda spoke to herself as she watched Clancy gun his engine and peel out, barely in time to see Angel top the hill. "Didn't tell him nothin'. Wouldn't tell him the time of day to save his sorry hide. Wouldn't throw him a life ring if he was drownin' in the river. But I'd help Angel . . . and she needs to get this mess settled once and for all and get on with her life, so there!"

The housekeeper set her broom against the house, sat down in the swing and smiled.

Angel was on her knees in the fenced enclosure at the far east side of the little cemetery, when she looked up and saw him standing just outside the gate. "What in hell are you doing here?" she demanded. "Get out right now, Clancy. I mean it with all my heart, soul, and mind. Get out of my life."

"No. We're going to talk," he said slowly. "We can do it over dinner tonight. We can do it right here. You name the place. Is this where your grandmother is buried?" He read the name on the center granite stone, *Dorothy June Conrad, 1912-1991*, then turned and read the one to her right, *John Herman Conrad, 1910-1960*. Before he could look at the one to the left, Angel was standing in front of the tombstone, shielding it.

"I'm not talking to you. Not today or ever," she declared.

"What happened, Angel? Did you marry someone? Did you have our baby and give it away or did you keep it? God, I thought you'd embarrass me and tell everyone in Tishomingo it was mine, but you didn't. Then you were gone and I was so relieved . . . but now—"

"But now what?" She tried to will the tears to dry up, but they dripped down her cheeks.

"I want to know what happened. Angel, give me some answers."

She stepped to one side and sat down on the park bench beside the third tombstone. "There is your answer," she whispered.

And he read out loud, "Clancy Morgan Conrad, March 18, 1988."

"Your son was stillborn. Eight pounds, and so beautiful he would take your breath away, but he couldn't live—not any more than your love for me could live. Now you've got your answers, so go away, Clancy Morgan, and leave me alone," she said through clenched teeth.

Four

"Good mornin'," Patty greeted Angel when she opened the door to her office. "Have a good weekend?" She tossed her long, straight brown hair over her shoulder and opened another letter with a silver dagger.

"Had a helluva weekend." Angel took her sunglasses off, revealing red and swollen eyes. "I've cried buckets and buckets and Hilda has used every cuss word she knows both in English and Spanish."

"What happened?" Patty's brown eyes were round as saucers.

"Call the rest of the girls for a meeting in my office," Angel said, adding, "Just us, not the rest of the board." She opened the heavy double doors into her private office and poured steaming, hot coffee into a mug with the Conrad Oil Enterprises logo on the side. Bless Patty's heart, she was more than the best secretary in the world. She was also a good friend and she made powerful coffee.

"Okay," the five of them said in unison as they trooped into the office and pulled up chairs around the long conference table.

"Clancy followed the bus from Davis to Denison, and then he followed me across the river to Hendrix. I stopped the car and pointed my gun right at his nose, and I thought he'd turned around. But he kept after me all the way to the farm," she said dryly.

"Damn! Then what?" Patty asked.

"He followed me to the cemetery and now he knows everything," Angel told them. "I asked him to leave and never come back. After I showed him his son's tombstone, he hung his head and walked away. When I got back to my house, he wasn't there. So why the hell did I spend the whole weekend crying my stupid eyes out? He did just exactly what I told him to do."

Angel looked around the table at the faithful friends who had stood by her for all these years. They had all come a long way since she'd met Allie in the university library ten years ago this fall. Angel had been five months pregnant with Clancy's baby, and working on a geology assignment. The two young women became instant friends.

Before long Allie had introduced her to the rest of the gang, and every one of them had cried with Angel when the baby was stillborn.

Now, every one of her friends knew for a certainty that if their boss didn't get Clancy Morgan out of her heart, she would never be able to lead a full life.

After all, Angel almost never dated. The few times she had, she had turned tail and run when the fellow began to get the least bit serious.

"Damn him!" Mindy swore. "Just when I thought I had you on the right track. Just when you were starting to do some serious dating. Why did he have to come back in the picture now? Lord, we haven't got time for this. We've got a wedding to plan for Bonnie and a divorce for me to get through, and Lord knows Susan is going to wake up someday and say yes to Richie. Seems like he asks her to marry him at least once a week."

"And I'm pregnant," Allie said bluntly. "Guess there ain't no time like the present to announce it. We seem to be having a group confession."

"Well, hallelujah." Angel smiled and her eyes began to twinkle. "I'm glad to hear that. You aren't goin' to quit work, are you?"

"Hell, no. Next to you, I'm the best damn geologist in the great state of Texas and I'm not even thinkin' about quitting work. I'll strap my baby on my back and tell those drillers how to do their jobs, and my kid can grow up knowing everything there is to know about

oil wells," she said. "But what are you goin' to do if
he comes back again? He knows where you live and
where your company is," Allie said.

"I don't know. I thought it was all behind me. I
thought I could go back to that alumni banquet, strut
my stuff, show off the band and leave feeling fine, but
it didn't work that way. The minute I saw him my insides turned to jelly and that old ache was right back
in my heart," Angel told them. "I just wanted you all
to know the situation up front. I may be an old bear
these next few days, but it doesn't mean I'm upset with
any of you. And I don't know if he'll come walking
through the door at any time, and I'm not so sure I
want to see him if he does. One part of me still wants
to kiss him and the other part wants to watch him die
a slow and gruesome death."

"If you want to watch him die, I won't let him past
my part of the building." Susan gave her the thumbs-
up sign. "Don't worry. First office is my territory. If
he gets past me and my big, old double-barreled shotgun, then Mindy can head him off at the pass."

"Sure." Mindy nodded. "I'm in a bad situation. You
know this divorce stuff is for the birds. I've decided
sex is a misdemeanor. The more I miss, de meaner I
get. Clancy Morgan better not try to sweet talk his way
past my office or he'll find out he's dealin' with PMS
and abstinence all at the same time. Don't worry, we'll
toss him out of the second-floor window on his handsome face, and by then your insides won't turn to jelly
when you look at him."

Angel laughed and shook her head. It seemed like
such a big mountain this morning, but the girls were
whittling it down to the molehill it really was. "You're
good for me," she said. "Guess we better dry our tears

and run this oil business now. The big boys would just love to see me blubbering over a lost love, wouldn't they? They said I'd never make it in a man's world, but I've got you all. Six of us can outdo the work of a hundred men."

"Hell, one of us can outdo that many," Patty swore. "We'll manage, Angel. We've lived through marriages and rumors of marriages, war and peace, and I betcha this don't keep the sun from coming up, either."

Angel went back to her office and turned on her computer. It was time to get out of the rut she'd allowed herself to wallow in for the past two days, and to get back to work. That's what she needed—good, complicated, exhausting work to erase Clancy Morgan's face from her mind.

By noon she'd argued with the board of directors, had a meeting with Mindy concerning the wording on a multimillion-dollar contract, and met with Susan about advertising in *The Daily Oklahoman*. The phone rang, and Patty answered, "Conrad Oil Enterprises. May I help you?"

"Whoops." She put her hand over the receiver and pressed the intercom button into Angel's office. "Guess Susan is out to lunch. Seems like the monster has gotten past her double-barreled shotgun."

"What?" Angel whispered back.

"It's Clancy on the phone," Patty said. "Want me to tell him to drop dead or that I'm putting a contract out on his hide? How about I tell him you've left for a month on your honeymoon?"

"I'll talk to him," Angel said. "I hope he's been as miserable as I have."

"Yeah, for a whole weekend," Patty said sarcastically. "That isn't ten years, you know."

Angel frowned at Patty and shut the door between their offices.

"Hello, Clancy."

"Angela?" His voice sounded weary.

"Yes, this is Angel," she said.

"I owe you one helluva an apology. I'm so sorry. I'm miserable from it all, and I don't even know what to say. I've been a jackass and there's no excuse for what I did back then. I was just a scared kid and . . ." he stammered.

"And what?" she said. "Am I supposed to forgive you? Will that make you leave me alone?"

"I don't deserve your forgiveness, Angela," he said in a broken voice. "I don't deserve anything from you. I was prepared to meet a little kid that might look like me, or for you to tell me you'd given it away to a couple who couldn't have children. I would like to talk to you in person and then I promise I'll get out of your life and never bother you again."

"Is that a real promise or one of those like you used to make?" she asked.

"It's real, and it's coming from a broken heart," he said. "Can I meet you or pick you up for dinner?"

"Sure," she said. "If you'll promise you'll never, ever call me again. You can pick me up right here in my office at five o'clock this afternoon. But you'll have to be seen with me in public this time, since I don't think we've got time to go to Pennington Creek like we used to."

"I'll be there," he said tersely.

She punched the intercom and said, "Patty, tell Susan and all the girls to hold their fire. Clancy is com-

ing at five o'clock and I don't want a single shot in him
when he gets to my office. When he walks in, Susan is
to meet him at the door and take him back down the
hall . . . Mindy gets him there, and you know the rest.
I want him to see every office and talk to every one of
us before he gets up here. We're going to settle this
thing, and I'm going to get him out of my life and my
heart tonight. When the sun comes up tomorrow,
Clancy Morgan is going to be forgotten as far as I'm
concerned."

Patty hid a smile. She'd be willing to bet her brand
new pickup against a wagonload of horse manure that
by tomorrow Clancy would still be swaggering around
looking like a million dollars, and by the end of the
month, Angel would have a mended heart.

At five o'clock, he pushed the door open to the first
floor, and Susan met him with a fake smile plastered
on her face. "Mr. Morgan, I believe. Welcome to Conrad Oil Enterprises, Incorporated. My name's Susan.
I'm in charge of PR and advertising. Maybe you remember me from the alumni concert we gave last
week. I play the fiddle." She stuck out her hand and
shook his firmly, hoping to intimidate him.

"Who died and left this company to Angela?" he
asked bluntly.

"No one," Susan said "Follow me, please. Angel is
a top-notch geologist, and she knows as much about
the oil business as anyone. She majored in geology
and minored in business and she's a hell cat on wheels
when it comes to making deals. She played a hunch
right out of college and drilled a well on the property
she inherited from her grandmother. People all told

her she was crazy. There wasn't any oil in that part of the state. But she ignored them and bet every last cent she had on a hunch. It paid off, and then she invested the money wisely and, in a few months, she owned her own company. When the Texanna Red Oil Company wanted to move their base to Louisiana, they offered to sell this building to her, and she bought it."

"Hello, Mr. Morgan." Mindy met him at the open door to her part of the building. "These are our director's and lawyers' offices. Follow me, please. By the way, I want you to keep in mind that I could shoot you between the eyes and enjoy watching you die a slow and painful death," she said, in the same matter-of-fact tone she would've used to order a tunafish sandwich for lunch. "You've made Angel miserable and she's my best friend."

"I realize that, Mindy," he said. "Am I going to have to talk to everyone in Conrad Oil before I get to her?"

"Yup. That's the only way you get to the top in one piece and alive," she said. "Angel takes care of us all, and we take care of her. So you better watch your step or I'll dream up some crazy lawsuit to bedevil you with," she added sweetly.

Clancy just nodded.

"Hello, Clancy." Allie met him at the top of the stairs on the second floor. "So you're the infamous rich boy who—"

"Nice to meet you, too." He gritted his teeth. "This is ridiculous."

"But necessary," Allie said firmly. "Shall we continue the tour? This is the geology department, where we decide when, if, and where to drill. Angel spends a lot of time here since she's the only geologist in the whole state of Texas who has better intuition than I do. There's been times when my call would have netted us a million dollars worth of dry well. She's got a sixth sense when it comes to drilling. Too bad she doesn't have one when it comes to you."

He scowled, but said nothing.

"Clancy Morgan, I do believe." Bonnie took over next. "I'm glad to finally meet you and I think maybe I owe you a pat on the back. If you hadn't been such a rat to Angel ten years ago, not one of us would be where we are today. She's kept us together and we love her. So say what you have to, then back out of her life."

"If I ever get to see her," he said flatly. "I didn't know I had to run the gauntlet to reach the top floor. I thought I'd just ask where she worked, get on an elevator and find her office."

"Well, that's what you get for depending on your own shallow thinking," she said as she opened the door marked with a brass plaque that read *Angela Conrad, President.* "Patty, he's all yours," she said.

"Clancy, you S.O.B., come right in here and sit down," Patty said with a big smile. "Angel is on the phone to Maine and she'll be a little while."

She filed the sheaf of papers she'd been typing and sat down across the desk from him. "Why did you treat her so rotten anyway?"

"Because I was a scared eighteen-year-old kid who thought the whole world was Tishomingo, Oklahoma. I was stupid enough to believe that what people thought about me would either make or break me," he said honestly. "I've listened to all of your opinions all the way up from the bottom. Now let me ask you something. Why in the hell did she make me meet every one of you?"

"Because every one of us were with her the night she gave birth to your son. We timed the contractions for her when she was in labor, and held her hands when it was time to push. We were her cheerleading squad when the pains were so hard they took her breath away, and we cried with her when that little boy was stillborn. We all held him in our arms one by one, and offered to kill you to make it up to her. She wouldn't let us do it.

"So we just thought we'd get to know you, even though all she'll let us do now is walk with you from one office to the next. And if you talk your way back into her life and make her cry again, you're going to disappear—just like that. Someone might find you in six million years when they drill for oil . . . but it'll probably be a dry hole like your cold old heart."

She broke off abruptly when Angel appeared in the doorway.

"Clancy! Please come in."

After the treatment her girlfriends had put him through, Clancy was surprised to hear the genuine welcome in her voice. Patty threw him a warning look that Angel somehow missed, and made herself scarce. Angel chattered on nervously as Clancy sat down by her desk.

"I've got a few loose ends to tie up here and then we can go to dinner. Do you still like Mexican food? I know a little place where they serve the real stuff, but the spices will fry your innards, so I hope you like it hot," she finished up, feeling a little foolish. "So. Did the girls give you the official tour of Conrad Oil?"

"They sure did. I was impressed."

"Wonderful bunch, aren't they?" She closed a folder and shut down her computer. "Met them my first semester in college. That's when we formed the band. Played the honky-tonks and dives in those days for extra money to help pay our way through school. Lord knows, I never would have made it through that first year without them. They were the first real friends I ever had, and we've stayed together through thick and thin, marriages, divorces, tears, and giggles. There now, I think everything else can wait until tomorrow. Are you ready?"

"I'm ready." He smiled for the first time. "And I love Mexican. They can't make it too hot for this Okie."

"Elevator or stairs?" she asked as they passed Patty's desk.

"Elevator," he said bluntly. "I think I've had enough exercise for today."

The Mexican waitress seated them at the back of the restaurant, at Angel's usual table. "Margarita?" she asked.

"Iced tea for me," Angel unrolled the bandanna wrapped around the silver utensils and put it over her lap. "Clancy?"

"Iced tea is fine," he said.

"Now what do you want to talk about?" She picked up the menu and scanned it.

"Us. I still want to know what you've done this past ten years, even though your friends each filled me in a little," he said, then looked up at the waitress. "I'll have the chicken enchiladas. Do they come with refried beans and rice?"

"Yes, sir." The waitress nodded. "And a side order of hot vegetables and flour tortillas?" she asked Angel, remembering what her favorite customer liked.

"That would be good, Linda," Angel said. "Bring me the beef fajitas, a full pound tonight. I'm hungry."

"Yes, ma'am," she said, and disappeared into the kitchen.

"You're pretty persistent. I was hoping all your questions would be answered by now."

"How did you get started in the oil business?" he asked, ignoring her remark.

"My great-grandfather died just about the time you and Melissa went to Norman to college. He left us the farm, twenty acres of the prettiest green grass in the state. We left Tishomingo since we could live in Kemp rent free and it was closer to the university which had given me a grant and a scholarship. Guess you forgot about me telling you that," she said. "Anyway, four years later Granny died and I graduated with a major in geology and a minor in business. I had a hunch and drilled on the property. Everyone thought I was a fool, because there wasn't an oil well anywhere around Kemp, Oklahoma, but it turned out right and I was pretty well off overnight. Then I played a few more hunches and everything I touched turned to gold. The girls helped me a lot. Allie is a geologist, Mindy is a lawyer, and Bonnie is a wizard at accounting."

"And Susan is great at PR with everyone but me, and Patty is a top-notch secretary who would like to feed my heart to the buzzards," he finished for her.

"You can't blame them," she defended her friends.

"I guess not, if I'm honest. And while we're being honest, I've got a couple of things to tell you. That night you told me you were pregnant I wanted to sit down and promise you the moon, but my mother and father would have died if I'd come home and told them I'd gotten you pregnant. Not to mention Melissa. I'd already proposed to her. We got married the week after we graduated, and she taught school while I was in the Air Force. Until one fine day when she announced she wanted to split so she could marry the principal at her school. I moved out, filed for divorce, and came home. End of story.

"I tried my best not to think about you, Angel. When I did, it was with a sigh of relief that you hadn't made a fuss and a fool out of me. Now I know I made myself a fool. I loved you as much as a stupid kid can love anyone."

Angel looked everywhere but at him, and Clancy continued.

"Melissa only looked perfect. She was the cheerleader and the right girl from the right family who would know all the right things to say and do. She was also cold in the bedroom. She wasn't warm like you and she didn't make me feel like a million dollars the way you always did. At first I thought I just didn't know better because I'd only been with you and then her by the time we were in college a few months. But I've been with other women since then, and it's never been the same feeling I had on the creek bank with you. Not even close."

She managed to look at him, but her expression was unreadable. Clancy wondered if he'd said too much.

"Well, enough soul cleansing," Angel said as the waitress put the hot platters of food in front of them. "You know my story and now I know yours. But there isn't a future for us today, any more than there was that hot August night ten years ago. It's over, Clancy. We've both grown up and there's nothing left for us. Besides, it takes trust to build a relationship and I wouldn't trust you as far as I could throw you."

Five

Clancy drove back across the Red River to Oklahoma. He stopped in Durant at a liquor store and bought two six-packs of beer and a pint of Jack Daniel's, then went to Tishomingo meaning to drown his sorrows, somehow, even if it was childish and not one damned thing would be accomplished when the sun came up tomorrow morning. It had been years since he'd been drunk, and tonight he intended to get so plastered that by morning his head would feel like a drum was keeping time inside it and then maybe he wouldn't think about Angela.

"Hey, Clancy!" his mother called from the kitchen when she heard him open the door. "I had salad with the ladies at the country club. Have you eaten?"

"Yep." He nodded. "But I'm going out again to do a little fishing. Probably won't be back until morning."

"Okay. I've got to make phone calls about the auxiliary picnic next week." His mother came into the living room. "I've got a hairdresser's appointment in the morning at nine, so please be quiet if you come in late." She smiled, showing beautiful white teeth. Meredith Morgan worked at keeping both her figure and her skin flawlessly young, and it was easy to see where Clancy had gotten his good looks.

He went down the hall to the bedroom which had been his since he was a baby. He changed from navy-blue pleated dress slacks and a pinstriped shirt into a pair of cut-off shorts and a faded tank top, kicked his good loafers in the floor of the closet and pulled on a pair of grungy white tennis shoes with no laces. "See you later," he called as he left the same way he'd come in, noticing that his mother did take a moment to look up from the phone and wave at him.

He parked the Bronco near Pennington Creek, took an old blanket out of the back, and tucked it under his arm. He shuffled the beer and the bourbon until it fit under his other arm and plodded down the pathway to the sandbar. He fought the brambles back under the trees until he found the very spot where he and Angel had lain together so many times, and carefully spread out the blanket, scaring away a frog and a grass snake while he was at it. Then he picked up the first six-pack of beer and went to soak his feet in the edge of the water. He wanted to try and remember the good times while his brain was still lucid.

Clancy popped the top on the first can and guzzled about half the contents before he came up for air. He hummed a few bars of a song until he remembered the lyrics . . . something about a man who'd never been happy until he had a wife and kids. He tilted the can back and let the rest of the beer slide down his throat in one big swallow.

He sang the rest of the lyrics at the top of his lungs, off-tune and off-key, just to make himself feel worse. He popped the tab on another silver can and continued to sing, until a sudden thought stopped him cold.

"I could've had a wife and kids," he whispered to himself. "But I threw it all away because of my pride and my fears. Well, here's to all the mistakes made by all the young proud fools in the whole state of Oklahoma in the last ten years." Clancy opened the third can of beer and started sipping it slowly.

He had almost finished the first six-pack by eleven o'clock and his fishing equipment was still in the back of the Bronco. He lay on his back, his feet in the water and beer cans stacked in a crazy pyramid next to him, and watched the moon rise, and thought of another song. He started to hum and whisper the words. "Try . . . try . . . hmmmm . . . try to remember why we fell in love."

"Hello," a feminine voice said to his right.

"Angel?" he didn't even look. The sound of her voice was probably just a drunken illusion, but even if it was an illusion, maybe he could carry on a make-believe conversation with her.

"Who?" the voice asked, annoyed.

"Angel?" he repeated without taking his bleary eyes off the moon.

"Look at me, Clancy. God almighty, did you drink all these beers? What in the hell do you think you're doing? You're a grown man with a responsible job. The high school principal would probably fire you on the spot if he knew you were lying down here in the dirt half-crocked."

He turned and looked at his ex-wife, Melissa, sitting on the sandbar beside him. Well, wasn't this just funnier than the time the preacher sat on the cake at the church social. He hadn't seen her in three years, not since their day in court. What a helluva time for her to show up. He noticed a few wrinkles around her eyes and her blond hair was shorter than he'd ever seen it. Other than that she was the same old Melissa, looking as if she'd just walked out of *Vogue*. He impulsively looked down at her feet . . . Yep, her toenails were showing at the ends of her sandals and they were freshly polished. How many times had he been ready to go somewhere and had to wait for Melissa's toenails to dry before they could leave?

"Your mother said you might be down here fishing," she said. "I just thought I'd drop by."

"And what, Melissa?" he asked. "What in the hell are you doin' here?"

"I come home every summer for a week to see Momma and Grandma, remember?" she said. "Since we got divorced you've never been here when I am," she explained.

"Have a beer?" He held up a full six-pack, still held together with the plastic webbing.

"You know I hate beer," she snarled.

"Then grab that bottle of bourbon under that tree bough and we'll drink to the good old days," he laughed sarcastically.

"You're drunk," she snarled again.

"And you're married," Clancy reminded her. "I'll get the damned bourbon. Never let it be said I was a bad host at my own self-pity party, even if you are an uninvited guest." He slurred the last word and wobbled just a little bit when he stood up. The sandbar swirled slightly and the moon dropped about six feet toward the horizon, but he didn't fall. He staggered back to the blanket.

"Here's the stuff." He sat down, carefully, stuck his wrinkled feet back in the water and flopped back on his back to stare at the stars again. "Sorry, can't give you a crystal glass to drink it out of. Just tip the bottle back and drink it straight."

"What's gotten into you?" she asked. "You never drank," she reminded him. "You always were the designated driver in high school and you wouldn't even drink a glass of wine with me on our first anniversary."

"You wouldn't understand." He worked hard to make his words come out right.

"Did I do this to you, Clancy?" she whispered dramatically.

He chuckled down deep. The chuckle soon became a laugh, and he sat up to wipe his eyes with the back of his hand.

"Oh, Clancy." She shook her head. "You were so brave through the divorce. I never knew I caused you this much grief. Have you been drinking ever since?"

"Hell, no!" He raised his voice loud enough to be heard all the way across the creek.

"You poor man. I'm so sorry," she sighed.

"You ought to be." Clancy sat up slightly then fell back on his old blanket again. "You ought to be sorry, because you never did love me. You never loved anybody but yourself, Melissha." He heard himself slur her name and made a mental note to work harder at keeping his words straight, because he damned sure intended to tell her what he thought about her while she was sitting there, acting like a soap opera star.

"Oh, Clancy, I loved you," she retorted.

"Oh, sure, but it really don't matter a whole helluva lot, now, Meliss . . . a," he was proud of himself for not slurring. "Because I didn't love you, either. I just married you because everyone thought that's what we should do. You had the wedding planned and there were all those showers and presents, and I knew I'd be considered a real heel if I backed out of the marriage then. You know who I really loved? I loved Angela Conrad," he said.

"You're full of it," she said, gracefully enough. "You couldn't love her. She was just poor white trash and she's probably off somewhere with a house full of snotty kids—"

"Angel owns Conrad Oil Company in Denison, Texas," he said, as clearly as if he were stone-cold sober. "She's not white trash and never was."

"Oh, she's Angel now, is she? Well, you didn't love her. You were in love with me from the eighth grade," she reminded him.

"Nope, I wasn't. Remember the summer after we graduated? You told me that you thought I was acting funny. Distant, you said, and you asked me if I still loved you," Clancy reminded her.

"Sure." Melissa nodded, flipping back her blond hair, cut in a short pageboy. "You had the senior blues. Graduation was over. Football season was done. College hadn't started. Momma said you'd be all right when we went to college, and you were."

Clancy didn't answer for a while. The six beers were wearing off faster than he thought they would, and he wasn't looking forward to the headache tomorrow morning—even if he did deserve it.

"Melissa, that whole summer I was seeing Angela Conrad behind your back. You said you loved me but you wouldn't let me—"

"Oh, hush," she said.

"Well, you let me take off most of your clothes, but then you wouldn't go the final step and make love with me," he said. "So I took you home and came down here to go skinnydipping, and cool off. Angela was sitting right here on this sandbar, all alone. We talked until three o'clock in the morning and then I took her home. The next night I took you home and came back. She was here again, and before long she was giving me what you just teased me with. Only I was young and stupid and didn't realize the girl was in love with me."

"You did *what?*" she screamed at him. "You were making it with her after you took me home?" She slapped his face, sobering him even more.

"Don't hit me again, Melissa," he warned in an icy tone. "Don't ever hit me again. I'm just tellin' you what happened. I made wild, passionate love with her, and it was damned good. Better than any I ever made with you."

"You bastard." She stood up and shook the sand off the bottom of her khaki walking shorts. "How dare you cheat on me before we were married!"

"How dare you cheat on me after we were married?" His tone was even colder. "Guess we're about even, for what it's worth."

"Shut up!" she said.

"Angela got pregnant," he said. "I came down here that hot August night a week before we were to go to college. I was going to tell her I wasn't coming back any more no matter what, and she told me she was pregnant with my child. Know what I told her? I didn't stand beside her and face the wrath of my parents and yours. Oh, no, I was the biggest chicken of all time. I told her to marry Billy Joe and I walked away from her as if she was nothing to me."

"Why are you telling me this now?" Melissa asked, outraged.

"Because you need to know you're not the reason I'm trying to get drunk tonight. I don't give a damn about you. I'm still in love with Angela—Angel—and she won't have a thing to do with me, because I ran out and left her. My son was stillborn, Melissa, and I didn't even care enough to find out until now."

"Good-bye, Clancy," she said. "I hope you rot in hell. Does your mother know this? She's always hoped you and I would get back together. So evidently she hasn't got a clue. But she will tomorrow, Clancy. Because if you don't tell her, I will."

"Bet you would just love to do that, wouldn't you?" he laughed heartily. "Go ahead."

Melissa stomped off in the sand, not making a noise as she left, until she got into her car by the road. Then she lay down some smoking rubber as she squealed the tires in anger. Clancy pulled his feet from the water and looked at the wrinkled skin while he finished sobering up. So much for getting drunk and singing sad songs tonight, or for shutting the door on his past failures and secrets. But what the hell, at least Melissa hadn't gone away with a lilt in her step, thinking he was still madly in love with her and letting him corrode his liver to prove it.

Clancy sat for hours, until he'd sobered up all the way. He gathered up his blanket, tossed the unopened bottle of bourbon in the back of the Bronco with the last six-pack of beer and started back home to tell his mother what had happened. At least that way she wouldn't find out at the beauty shop tomorrow morning.

"Hello, Clancy." His mother was watching an old movie on late-night television when he crossed the living room and sat down in his dad's leather recliner next to her. She had on one of those mask things that made her face all green and cracked looking, and her hair was wrapped up in a towel. "Did Melissa find you? I told her you'd gone fishing. You know that girl comes to see me every year when she comes to visit her relatives. She says she still feels like I'm her mother-in-law. I think she regrets the way your marriage ended. I hope you wouldn't be silly enough to give her a second chance. I think she thinks I still like her, can you believe it?" She spoke without taking her eyes from the movie. "Good Lord," she finally noticed Clancy's feet. "What did you do? Fish barefoot in the water all evening?"

"Nope. I put my feet in the water and then I laid back and watched the moon come up. I tried my damnedest to get sloppy drunk, but it didn't work," he said honestly.

"Drunk?" Her eyes were round with awe. "You?"

"Yep, me," he said. "Mother, I've got something I want to tell you. The summer after my senior year I was sneaking around with Angela Conrad . . ."

"Not Dotty Conrad's granddaughter," she looked at him seriously.

"Yes, that's the one." He nodded. "I fell in love with her but I was too young and stupid to realize it. Besides, I couldn't tell you and dad . . ."

"But, why? Dotty might not have had money, but she was a fine woman. And Angela was probably the nicest little girl I ever met. Remember, Dotty used to clean house for me? Angela came with her lots of times. But then maybe you didn't know that. That was when you and your dad usually went to Texas to do 'boy things.' Anyway, Angela didn't come with her after she was about sixteen. Dotty said she was cleaning somewhere else so they could make more money."

"Good grief, you mean she was our hired help?" Clancy exclaimed.

"Sure. She dusted and ran the vacuum lots of times for Dotty," his mother said.

"Mother, she was pregnant at the end of the summer," he said bluntly, "and I ran out on her. I was scared she'd embarrass me and you and dad."

"You did what?" His mother's brown eyes sized him up and Clancy suddenly felt all of two feet tall. "I didn't raise you to be uncaring and selfish."

"No, you didn't," he agreed. "I did it on my own."

"Do I have a grandchild?"

"No, my son was stillborn. I didn't find out about it until this week, and now I realize I'm still in love with Angela. Of course, she doesn't want anything to do with me!" he said miserably.

Meredith Morgan had never seen her son so unhappy. Of all the crazy twists life could take. She'd been worried about what everyone in town would say when they found out she'd begun dating again, and now the buzz at the beauty shop tomorrow morning would undoubtedly center on Clancy.

"Since you've been honest with me . . ." his mother held her breath for a minute. "I've been seeing a man."

Clancy jerked his head around to stare at her. His dad had been right up there next to the angels in Clancy's eyes and the very thought of someone else with his mother made his stomach knot up. He'd dreaded this day since the day of his dad's funeral when he overheard two local gossips saying something about his mother being young enough, pretty enough, and Lord knew, rich enough to find another husband before long. "You what? Who?"

"Tom Lloyd," she said.

"You're kidding me," he gulped.

"I'm quite serious."

"But, Mother, he's beneath you," he said. "He's—"

"Right." She nodded. "Tom's the maintenance supervisor at the cemetery. His wife died the same year your father did, and he's been lonely, too. Clancy, I don't need money and I really don't give a damn about hanging around that fancy country club. What I want is someone to love me and to spend time with me."

Clancy blinked away years of snobbery in a few seconds. "Then why don't you ask him to dinner while I'm here?" he said.

"Thanks, son." She patted his arm. "Maybe I will. Guess you're more like me than I thought. Now, tell me, where again is it that Angela lives? And how did she get so rich as to own an oil company? Did you tell her that we used to own part of Texanna Red until your dad died and Red bought back the shares?"

"Hell, no!" he said. "And I didn't tell her that Red wants me to work for him, either. But I don't want to work in oil, and I love teaching, even if my paycheck isn't nearly what my oil investment check is each month. I don't love Conrad Oil. Like you said, I don't need money. I need Angel . . . and I've realized it too damned late!"

Six

Patty had had all she intended to put up with by the next Monday morning. Angel hadn't mentioned Clancy from Tuesday through Friday and Patty knew he hadn't called once all that week. But Angel's green eyes were as sad as they were the day they had gathered around the black hole in the Kemp cemetery that was her grandmother's final resting place. It was time for Angel to either kiss him or kill him and get on with living her life, and if no one else was going to prepare his wedding or his funeral, then Patty would take matters in her own hands—even if it made Angel mad.

Even facing her best friend's anger would be better than this damned cloud hanging over their heads while Angel went around sighing and saying she had buried all her memories and told her first love they didn't have a future together. But it was clear that she couldn't stop thinking about him, and Patty was pretty sure Clancy was thinking about Angel, too.

She crossed one long, stockinged leg over the other one, and tugged the bottom of a lemon yellow miniskirt down to cover at least another inch of her muscular thigh. She pushed the red button on the intercom at the edge of her desk. "Mayday," she whispered, and four other women stopped what they were doing and ended up in the conference room on the second floor.

"What's up?" Allie looked a little green above her upper lip. The doctor said she could expect the morning sickness to stop in three months and she sure hoped he knew what he was talking about. If this nausea lasted the whole nine months, Tyler could accept the idea of an only child or have the next one himself and see just how much he enjoyed feeling like he was going to hurl his food at any given time. "Where's Angel?" She rolled her eyes at the chocolate chip cookies on the table.

"She's having breakfast with Red and Anna to talk about their company moving their main office back here. Red would like to talk her out of this building. Says his crew hates Louisiana and wants to come home to Texas," Patty said. "Sit down and let's make a decision. We don't have all day. She'll be back in a little while. We all know Angel is out of it these days. Lord, I can't work with her in this weird mood another day. It's like living with a zombie. I vote we send her on a vacation."

"Sure." Susan ran her hands through short red hair and laughed. "It'd be easier to set up a snow-cone stand in hell."

"We could run the company for two weeks, but she'll never go away." Bonnie did a rat-a-tat-tat on the table with her long fingernails. "You got something in mind, Patty?"

"Well, I do," Mindy butted in. "I vote we give her two weeks off for an early birthday present. She'll be twenty-eight at the end of the month and we've retired the band, so there's no reason she can't go. Now, where were you thinkin' about sending her, Patty?"

Patty smiled, and her eyes twinkled with excitement. "Panama City Beach, Florida. I know it's not as fancy as New Orleans or Paris, France, but it's calm down there. Remember when Ronald and I were keeping company and went there for a weekend. Lord, it was wonderful. And so quiet."

"Sounds like a great place for two people to fall in love all over again," Allie giggled. "I hope to hell Angel can't see through you as well as I can," she said.

Patty gave them all an innocent look. "Me? Why, I just thought our dear friend needs to relax. But not by herself." She smiled. "Suppose a tall, handsome fellow who filled out his jeans real well, and who just happens to know her from high school . . . well, what if he happened to show up on the beach at the same time that she did? Angel couldn't blame me for that now could she?"

"And it's time she took him back or set him free," Allie said. "She'll be here in a few minutes. Let's take her to dinner and tell her it's a done deal. You already got the plane tickets and plans made, Patty?"

"I'll do it," Bonnie said. "I can have everything ready at six o'clock. Let's go out for Italian food, and tell Angel she can have tomorrow to get things packed and ready. She can fly out of Dallas Wednesday morning, and we'll even let her take a laptop. But she can only call in once a day unless it's a dire emergency. Who's informing Clancy?"

"Not me," Susan said. "I'm no good at tellin' lies or keepin' secrets."

"Well, this is too important to leave to amateurs," Bonnie said. "I'll call him and then if she ever finds out, I'll blame it on Red."

All four women turned to look at her questioningly. She shrugged. "I found out Clancy's father was in the oil business with Red at one time. And I can keep a straight face when I lie." She smiled. "After all, I deal with the IRS."

"Why are we doing this?" Allie asked. "We've wanted to shoot Clancy dead for ten years and now here we are making arrangements to tell him where Angel is for two weeks. Not one damned bit of this makes a whole lot of sense to me."

"Angel's not happy," Patty said. "And the only thing that's goin' to make her happy is getting him either out of, or into, her heart. It's a love-him-or-leave-him kind of situation. So we're just helping her get her life straightened out so we can get on with ours. We've got a baby to birth in a few months, a wedding to stage, and a divorce to finalize. I move we get Angel's love life back on track, so we can do all that and more. And get back to running this oil business, too."

"I second the motion," Susan said. "Let's all agree before anyone chickens out. Meeting adjourned. See you all later." She passed the window looking down on Main Street as she moved toward the door. "Here she comes up the street. Better look sharp now and get back to work."

At five-thirty, they closed the front door and walked three blocks down Main Street to the Italian restaurant. When the waitress seated them at the back of the restaurant and brought a menu, Angel's funny feeling surfaced again and she knew that there was something going on and everyone else at the table knew all about it. She looked at Susan's face first, knowing full well she couldn't keep a secret in a bucket with a lid on it. Angel couldn't remember the last time Patty's eyes twinkled like that, as her friend tried to hide behind the menu, and just as she shifted her gaze to Mindy, she caught her winking at Allie. Bonnie was the only one who didn't act like she was sitting on a keg of dynamite with a short fuse.

Angel had to smile. "Okay. 'Fess up. What's going on?"

They all looked at Bonnie, who produced a big yellow envelope. "Surprise!" she said with a grin. "We've got an early birthday present for you. Lord knows you deserve it, but you wouldn't think of doing it for yourself, so we bought it for you. You're going to Panama City Beach, Florida, for two weeks, to a deluxe beachfront motel. Your room has a balcony overlooking a lake which is full of turtles, so you can feed them for excitement. And if your heart doesn't fail you after a thrill like that, you can put on your bathing suit, walk across the street to the beach and bask on the sand until some knight in shining armor comes racing dawn the beach on his big white four-wheeler and steals your heart away. But remember, it's only for two weeks. If he wants you to run off to a castle in France, the answer is no, because at the end of two weeks, you've got to come back to Conrad Oil and go back to work!"

Angel's eyes misted and her heart melted.

"You're all sweethearts." She wiped her eyes with the big white cloth napkin. "But the answer is no. I can't stand to be away from you all for that long."

"Bull," Patty said. "And we didn't ask a question so you can't answer no. You're goin' to be on that plane if I have to hogtie you and hire Mel Gibson to come throw your body over his shoulder and put you in the plane seat. You need to unwind. There's plane tickets, reservations for the motel, and I took your business papers out of your briefcase and put in three trashy romance novels. You're goin' home tonight to pack and we don't want to see your face at the office until two weeks from Wednesday. I'll even drive you to the airport."

"Everything's taken care of." Bonnie handed her the envelope. "Happy birthday, Angel. Go down there and find a handsome guy to make your eyes sparkle and your heart float. You've got all the money you'll ever need, so you don't have to look for a rich man. A gorgeous beach bum that thinks your bottom is gold-plated will do."

"Thanks a lot," Angel said wryly.

Angel had never been on a vacation that didn't involve the oil business. She'd flown all over the United States and abroad, but had never dreamed of doing anything this self-indulgent. Lie on a beach somewhere with a trashy book and read to her heart's content? It was all too tempting after the emotional upheavals of the past week, but impossible.

"Now you know I love you all—" she started.

"Good," Allie butted in. "That's all the thanks we need to hear. I vote we order a bottle of sparkling wine now to celebrate. Even if I can't drink it. I'm taking two weeks off when this baby is born and I betcha Bonnie's going to ask for a couple of weeks off for a honeymoon soon, so now it's your turn and you can't say no. We love you, too," she finished, a little out of breath.

Angel suddenly decided to give up arguing. She reached for the envelope and promised herself mentally that she would indulge her well-meaning friends and go—but she'd only stay until Sunday and fly back home in time for work on Monday morning.

"Okay, okay. You're all wonderful and I guess you won't let me refuse," she said ruefully. "Just tell me what color hair and eyes this gorgeous beach bum should have."

"Black hair and blue eyes, and he has to worship you like you're a goddess," Bonnie said seriously. "I think I'll have the lasagna, and to hell with my diet for tonight. I may eat fried ice cream afterwards, too."

"Hear, hear!" Allie raised her water glass in a toast. "Well, I'm eating for two even if y'all can't tell yet. So I'm having rigatoni and hot bread and I hope it doesn't come right back up!"

Angel's hunch wasn't satisfied. Something still wasn't right with this picture. She and her friends never kept secrets from each other and yet Susan's expression told her there was something she still wasn't telling. Why did they want her out of the office for two weeks?

It was midnight when Bonnie dialed the number she'd found in the old Texanna Red files. The phone rang five times before an older woman answered in a sleepy voice.

"Clancy Morgan, please," Bonnie said in her most businesslike tone.

"Who is this?" Meredith asked bluntly. "Do you realize it's midnight?"

"Yes, ma'am," Bonnie said. "Sorry about that. Unavoidable circumstances, you see. And this phone call involves Angel Conrad. Could I talk to Clancy or would you please give me his phone number?"

"My son's here and I'll wake him," Meredith said. "Has something happened to Angela?"

"No, ma'am," Bonnie said, but didn't offer more. In a few minutes, Clancy answered the phone.

"Angel?" his voice was taut with fear.

"Hello, Clancy. This is Bonnie," she said. "We met at the office. I'm the one in the accounting division."

"Is Angel all right?" he asked.

"She's fine except her heart is still broken after ten years. Lord, she should've gotten over you a long time ago, but she hasn't. Much as we'd like to, we can't fix her heart for her. Shooting you wouldn't even fix it," Bonnie said.

"Why are you calling me?" Clancy asked.

"I'm calling you to tell you that Angel is going on a two-week vacation to Panama City Beach, Florida. Get a pencil and take down this information. She'll fly out of Dallas on Wednesday morning at seven. Got that?"

"Why?"

"Why what?"

"If you hate me so much, why are you telling me this?" Clancy grabbed a pen and jotted down the information on the back of the telephone book on the nightstand beside his bed.

"Because we love Angel and she's got to either kiss you or kill you. And we want her back . . . with you if that's what it takes to make her happy. . . . Or without you, if she can shake you out of her heart once and for all. But all you've got is two weeks, and what happens is up to you. We don't really give a damn about *you*, Clancy. We just want Angel to be happy, and we think this is the only way we can make that happen," Bonnie said. "And if you tell her about this call, I'll swear you're lying. And I don't have to tell you which one of us she'll believe."

"Thanks," Clancy said, his heart beginning to feel lighter than it had in several days. "I'll catch a plane out of Oklahoma City on Wednesday morning, and I'll call for reservations in the same motel. And I'll do my best."

"Two weeks, Clancy. That's all you've got." Bonnie hung up the phone with a bang.

Seven

Angel parked her rented Ford Taurus in front of the motel, yanked one of the three suitcases from the backseat and stopped to smell the salt breeze that floated across the water and whipped her unruly brown curls around her face.

The sky was pure blue and there wasn't even one white cloud drifting over the water. The sand was as white as a new bride's veil, and suddenly she was glad she had agreed to a few days away from work, stress, and thoughts of Clancy. She was going to lie on the beach until dark, then soak in a tub of hot water and read one of the trashy books Patty put in her briefcase from beginning to end. And do nothing of importance.

"Hello," she greeted the man behind the desk. "I'm Angel Conrad and I've got reservations for the next couple of weeks."

"That's right." He smiled. "Room 214, upstairs, with a lake view at the back. Lots of turtles, but they keep quiet." He handed her the key and motioned to the colorful advertising flyers lined up neatly on the east wall. "Let us know if you'd like information about local attractions."

"Thank you." She took the key but didn't stop to pick up any brochures. Playing miniature golf or renting a sailboat wasn't what this vacation was all about. She was here to say her goodbyes to memories which had haunted her for ten years. Before she left this place on Sunday night, she planned to stand barefoot in the sand and let go of every single one of them into the ocean wind.

Evidently she'd been guilty of wearing her heart on her sleeve these past days and her friends had realized she needed some time to straighten out her life. Well, it *would* be straight come Monday morning, and they wouldn't ever have to worry about her again.

Angel went up the stairs to room 214 and plopped the suitcase down on the bed, then went back down to the car for the rest of her luggage. The office door was open and someone else was at the desk. She could hear the clerk telling him the same things he'd just told her with the same intonation, the same smile, the same wave of the hand, like a puppet on a string. The new guest looked vaguely familiar from the back, but she shrugged. She certainly didn't know anyone in Florida.

She kicked the unlocked door open with her foot and wrestled the rest of her baggage into the room, past the galley kitchenette and onto the king-sized bed. She opened the door to the bathroom and turned on the hot water, shucked out of her clothes and took a long shower to ease the tension out of her muscles.

Angel wrapped herself in a big white towel and
moved all the suitcases from the bed to the floor, then
collapsed on top of the blue-and-white floral bed-
spread, and let out a contented sigh. She propped up
on both pillows and grabbed the phone to call Patty,
but she changed her mind and put the phone back.
This was supposed to be a vacation, and she'd vowed
on the plane that she would not call Conrad Oil once
in the five days she planned to stay in Florida—instead
of the two weeks her friends had expected her to stay.

She unlatched one suitcase and found a bright red
bathing suit, a white terry cover-up, and a pair of white
leather thong sandals. After all, she hadn't come to
the beach to hole up in her room. She had to get out
on the sand and at least catch sight of one gorgeous
hunk to tell the girls about next week. It didn't matter
if he never said a word to her—she could make up
some kind of wild tale to entertain them over a glass
of wine.

She had the doorknob in her hand and was about
to turn it when a loud knock on the other side startled
her. She jerked the door open to find a tanned young
man with a smile that would make Patty swoon, and
he was carrying a gorgeous flower arrangement.

"Delivery for Miss Conrad," he said and handed
her a crystal vase with a dozen red roses interspersed
with white baby's breath. "Have a nice day now and
don't forget your sunblock. Fair as you are, you'd burn
in an hour on a day like this," he cautioned, and left
before she could say anything.

"Those girls!" Angel sighed, as she sat the flowers
on the glass-topped table for two in the kitchenette.
Then she opened the envelope holding the card attached to the red satin bow around the vase.

Yesterday, today, forever, She didn't recognize the handwriting and the card wasn't signed.

"Well," she said aloud. "Allie always was one for mystery. Probably trying to make me think there's someone here who's after my heart. Maybe he'll be a dark-eyed, gorgeous model who can wiggle out of a tight Speedo so fast he'll make my head swim." She picked up her tube of sunblock, threw it in her beach bag, stopped long enough to inhale the fragrance of the roses and went to the beach.

Angel dropped her bag in the warm sand and took out an oversize towel. This end of the beach was quiet and the sand was as fine and white as granulated sugar. She sat down on the towel and scooped up a handful, letting it slip through her fingers. Then she remembered the delivery boy's warning and dusted the fine grains from her hands, took off her terry cover-up and began to smooth sunblock cream over her legs.

She rolled over on her stomach and took one of the romance novels out of her bag. A picture of a handsome cowboy in tight jeans and a gaudy western shirt decorated the front. A woman with improbably deep cleavage was draped over his arm, and the smoldering look in his eyes promised the reader a love story beyond all expectations. Patty probably didn't even know the author and had picked it out for the cover art. But whether the author could write or not didn't matter one bit to Angela. She intended to read the book from prologue to epilogue, and enjoy every overheated page just to keep the thoughts of Clancy at bay.

* * *

Clancy had heard the shower running in the room next to his, and he heard Angel flop on the bed, and sigh happily. He knew when the delivery man brought the roses to her door, and he watched her from an opening in the drapes when she went to the beach. He thought about waiting until tomorrow to let her know he was here in Florida, but then he remembered that he only had two weeks and every minute was important.

He changed into swimming trunks and put on a tank top and a pair of sandals. He threw a towel over his shoulder, took a deep breath and started toward the beach, not knowing whether she would kill him or kiss him . . . as Bonnie had said. But whatever Angel's reaction might be, it would beat this emptiness in his life these past weeks. He walked toward her.

Angel was wearing a red two-piece bathing suit, not as skimpy as the one she had in high school, but then, there was a bit more of her to cover. She wore a floppy straw hat and huge sunglasses, and was propped up on her elbows reading a paperback book. A young man strolled past her and Clancy knew if she had looked up, the guy would've started a conversation, but she seemed to be oblivious to everything except the book.

Clancy flipped his towel out right beside her and sat on it, looking out over the ocean. By the time Angel realized someone was that close to her, she had to smile. Maybe it would be the knight in shining armor the girls had teased her about. She could get her story ready for them right now and then relax for the rest of her vacation. A familiar scent drifted by . . . she'd smelled that cologne before. A long time ago . . . on the banks of Pennington Creek.

She jerked off her sunglasses and looked right into Clancy's eyes. And all the pieces of the puzzle tumbled into place. Damn it all to hell! Her friends weren't supposed to send her on a vacation and then tell Clancy where she was. She couldn't decide whether to fire them and watch them starve to death, or simply shoot them and get it over with quick. But one thing was for sure when she got back. Every one of them would be facing her wrath and it wasn't going to be a pretty sight. They'd never seen her really boiling angry, but they would soon. All five of them were going to see her breathe fire before Monday morning was over.

"Small world, isn't it?" Clancy's smile was bright.

"Which one of them called you and told you I was here?" she demanded furiously.

"Don't know what you're talking about." He didn't blink and there was a twinkle in his eyes that made her heart flutter.

"Yes, you do." Angel stood up, gathering her things and stuffing them into the beach bag. "I'm checking out of the motel right now and driving my rental car back to the airport. I'll be home by morning and my so-called friends will be facing the firing squad."

"Sit down, Angel." He patted the towel before she could yank it up. "You can't run from me forever. Stay and get to know me. I'm a man now, not the scared young boy who didn't know his own heart." He studied her for a moment. "But if you really want to stay angry, you can just tell me go to go to hell, and get on with your life," he said affably. "By the way, did you like the roses?"

"You sent them? Hell's bells!" she swore. "Did all of you plan this together?"

"No. I just happened to schedule my visit here around your vacation time," he said. "What a coincidence, huh? Hey, I understand you know Red and Anna. Bet you didn't know there they were my dad's friends." Clancy tried rather awkwardly to change the subject so he wouldn't have to tell her that Bonnie had called him.

"You mean Red is in on this, too?" Angel sat back down. "Did he tell you where I was?"

"No," Clancy said, truthfully enough. "But you and I are both here for two weeks. I don't mind."

"Well, I do," Angel said crossly. "Anyway, *you're* here for two weeks, but I'm on my way out of this place as soon as I can pack. Won't be too hard, because I haven't really unpacked."

He just looked at her sadly and Angel almost melted.

"Clancy, I came here to clear my mind, not to make more mistakes."

"Afraid of me, are you?" he challenged.

Hardly, she almost said aloud. A situation like this didn't faze her any. Angel had faced a pregnancy without a husband. She'd worked like a dog to get an education. She'd buried the last living relative she had, and helped her friends through so many hard times she couldn't count them on her fingers and toes.

Then she'd carved a successful oil business out of a few acres of land which everyone had told her was only good for corn and sweet potatoes, and she wasn't afraid to meet the devil in a dark alley at midnight. So if Clancy Morgan thought for one minute she was going to turn and run, he had another think coming.

"No, I'm not afraid of you. Not one bit. But I bet when this vacation is over, it'll be you who'll be in a hurry to get back, Clancy."

He merely shrugged, which infuriated her even more.

"Those roses were beautiful, but you and I know they'll die before our two weeks are over . . . just the way our love died," she tormented him.

"Then I'll buy you another dozen." Clancy smiled, feeling as if he'd won the first skirmish of the war, without knowing exactly why he felt that way. He thought he detected a slight softening in her tone, despite her angry words.

Angel snorted, found her book in the bag, and threw the tube of sunblock lotion at him. "You might be more tan than me, but you'll still burn in sun like this. Help yourself. I'm not going to play nurse for you if you blister." She flipped the romance novel open to the page she had been reading and ignored him.

"Sorry to hear that. But I can't reach my back, and it looks to me like you didn't get enough on your shoulders. Do you think we could call a truce long enough to help each other out?" he asked, enjoying the view of the bare nape of her neck and down her back over her well-rounded bottom. He didn't forget to check out her shapely legs, crossed primly at her ankles.

"Why not?" she said indifferently. If she concentrated hard on how much she hated him, she would definitely be over Clancy Morgan once and for all by the end of this vacation. Granny used to say the way to not crave chocolate bars was to eat them until you got so sick you upchucked. Well, Angel'd spend so much time with Clancy that in two weeks her heart would know what her mind already understood: that Clancy was still the same selfish good-for-nothing who'd left her crying on the sandbar. And then it would finally be over! ·

"Yes, ma'am," he said with relish, loving the thought of actually getting to touch his Angel again. He squeezed the lotion into his big hands and gently rubbed her shoulders and down her back to where her bathing suit top fastened.

It took every bit of her willpower to keep from gasping when his hands made contact with her bare skin. No man had ever made her feel what Clancy had long ago, and no one else's touch could make her heart flutter like this. Not that she had any immediate plans to tell him so. Or future plans.

"Want me to undo this snap and get your whole back, or just reach under it?" he asked, trying hard to keep his voice emotionless so she wouldn't know how just the feel of her skin affected him.

"Undo it," she said pertly. Let him cope with his hormones however he could . . . she was going to make it as hard for him as possible.

"All done." He finished slathering lotion over every inch of her bare skin and fastened her top back. "Would you return the favor, Angel? I'd appreciate it."

Angel rolled over and took the tube of sunblock from his hands, determined he wouldn't know that her hands were shaking at the mere thought of rubbing lotion onto his muscled back and legs. She walked on her knees until she was behind him, glad he couldn't see her eyes behind the sunglasses and couldn't hear the thumping of her heart over the sound of the ocean.

"Be still," she said when he turned his head to the left so he could look over his shoulder. "What do you intend to do for two whole weeks?" she asked, and immediately regretted saying it.

"Whatever you want to do," Clancy said honestly, looking out over the ocean and enjoying the sensation of her hands caressing his back. "Maybe I'll just sit right here and let you rub lotion on me for two weeks. It's a pretty wonderful feeling."

Angel slapped his shoulder. "Oh, hush. It'll take longer than two weeks to get to know me. I'm not that naive teenager who thought you hung the moon and stars. I don't have a trusting heart anymore."

"Angel, don't talk like that. You knew your mind when I didn't know mine. Hey, I think you missed a spot over there on my right shoulder. If I get a sunburn, you'll have to put up with my whining," he teased.

"Heaven forbid." She rubbed more sunblock on his shoulder. "Now lie down and take a nap or I can give you a big, thick romance novel to read. Sorry I don't have anything else to offer. My dear friends didn't think to send along a thriller."

"A nap sounds wonderful. Don't leave without waking me, though. I thought we'd have dinner at a seafood restaurant I saw on my way down the strip, then we'd play a round of miniature golf, and after that we'd get a bottle of wine and come back here to watch the tide come in." He outlined his plans for the rest of the day as he lay down, crossing his arms above his head and resting his face on the backs of his hands.

"Did Patty plan all that, too?" she asked.

"Nope," he mumbled and shut his eyes. But he didn't go to sleep, any more than she read the book that was open in front of her face.

Angel stared at the words but didn't see them. She alternated between waves of annoyance and sheer fear. Annoyance at her friends for pulling such a stunt, and fear of her own feelings. How had he lured her into planning activities for the next two weeks? Her mind told her it wasn't any big deal. There wasn't a reason in the world she couldn't keep company with Clancy that long, then walk away from him without a glance over her shoulder.

But her heart told her she'd already lost when she played this game the first time. Even though she was older and knew the rules a whole lot better, she still had a soft spot for Clancy Morgan. And her body seemed to be telling her she'd better be extra careful, because if it could override her heart and mind, it intended to spend a good part of the vacation snuggled up to Clancy in that king-size bed.

"Oh, no, you are not," Angel whispered out loud.

"Are not what?" Clancy whispered back without opening his eyes.

"I'm talking to my book," she lied.

"Oh." He smiled, turned his head and opened his eyes to look at her. "By the way, do the rules say I can't look at you?"

"I didn't make the rules. You and my so-called best friends did," Angel said tartly, turning the page she hadn't read. "I might warn you. I'm damned good at miniature golf, and I shoot a mean game of pool, too. Used to pick up a few dollars on bets in the student union during college days. No one would believe a woman could out-shoot those big, tough cowboys."

"Then we'll have to play pool before we leave here," he promised. "Have I told you in the last five minutes how gorgeous your eyes are when you're angry? They have flecks in them that glitter and glow."

"You can't see my eyes. I have on sunglasses," she pointed out. "Try another line."

"I can see your eyes anytime I want. I can see your body next to mine right now with my eyes closed. Both of them are forever branded into my thoughts. But I've got to admit, it's a lot better when you are really here beside me, Angela. Being with you is the most peaceful thing I've done in a long time." Clancy kissed her gently on the cheek, then laid his head back down and shut his eyes.

Eight

Angel grabbed the hem of the full skirt of a red-and-white checked strapless sun dress and drew a portion of it through a white plastic loop, showing off her left leg to the top of her thigh. She pulled her curls behind her ears with two long barrettes, slapped on a little bit of makeup and buckled a pair of white, leather sandals on her feet. She was dabbing perfume behind her knees and ears when she heard his knock on the door.

"You look lovely." His eyes said as much as his voice when he saw her.

"Thank you, sir. You don't look so bad yourself." Clancy's casual khaki slacks had a perfect crease ending at the tops of soft leather loafers, and the top two buttons of his polo shirt were left undone, showing a thicker tuft of soft dark-brown hair than he'd had ten years ago . . . and he smelled like heaven. He opened the door to a silver Cadillac for her and whistled as he walked around the car to his door.

He settled into the car seat, and slipped a tape of the Judds into the deck, singing the songs her band had performed that night at the alumni reunion. "They aren't as good as you are," he said, as he backed the car out and started driving east, toward the restaurant where he had made reservations.

"Oh, sure." She smiled. "The Judds are in Nashville making millions and I've sold my bus and broken up my band. You've got rocks for brains if you think I'm that good."

"So, I've got rocks for brains. You're making millions, too, and they still can't sing as well as you. You always did sing well. Remember when you used to harmonize with whoever was on the radio in my Camaro? I remembered that when I looked up there on that stage you were standing there like an angel appearing out of a cloud of smoke. Lord, I thought I'd die when I realized it was you standing there. When you hopped up there on the table in front of me, my mouth felt like it was plumb full of cotton. I wanted to say something, but I didn't know what to say. Why didn't you give us all some advance notice of what you've accomplished?" he asked.

"Why? I didn't need to advertise my success to all those people who never thought I'd amount to anything. Come on, Clancy. I was poor, but I wasn't dumb . . . except when it came to you," she told him. "Now where's this restaurant? I'm hungry. I always get hungry when I'm around water very long. You know, I think this sunblock lotion really does work. I'm not burned at all," she rambled on, and then felt annoyed with herself for doing it.

"Well, good." Clancy pulled the car up to a restaurant with an awning in front. He handed a valet the keys and opened the door for Angela. "I figured you'd marry Billy Joe. You should have seen my face when I read that he was gay. Goes to show how much I knew, huh?"

The waiter showed them to a table for two on a wharf overlooking the ocean. A salty breeze blew the linen tablecloths and caused the candles, set down in deep crystal sconces, to flicker. He ordered the steak and shrimp special and she ordered a crab salad, with a side order of fried clams and shrimp with red sauce.

"Nice place," she commented when the waiter brought two tall glasses of iced tea and left with their orders.

"Best I could do on short notice. I'll study the brochures and see if I can come up with something a little more elaborate tomorrow night. There's a dinner cruise aboard a ship that goes out to Shell Island, but it was fully booked tonight. But we can go another time. Takes most of the afternoon, then we'll eat dinner and spend an hour on this island before we return. Sounded kind of romantic. Then there's another restaurant the clerk said was good that I thought we'd try tomorrow night. Unless, of course, you want to decide . . ."

Angel looked out at the setting sun's reflection in the water and thought she could probably come to this place every night for two weeks. Even if Clancy decided where they would eat every night, they'd still get on their separate airplanes and go back to Oklahoma. If at the end of two weeks, Clancy Morgan asked her to go to Tishomingo and eat at the Dairy Queen in front of all his home town friends, then she might be really impressed.

"Surprise me," Angel said, without looking at him. Two dolphins arched up out of the ocean and made graceful dives back into the water. "Did you see that?" she gasped. "It was absolutely beautiful."

"Not as beautiful as you," he said honestly, having a hard time taking his eyes from her bare shoulders and graceful neck. Lord, he would love to nuzzle in the softness below that strapless dress, but he knew it would take several days before he could even begin to think in terms of a physical relationship, no matter how badly he wanted to feel her warmth next to him. Hell, he might finish two weeks of heartache and long, cold showers, then fly back to Oklahoma without one single kiss. The only thing Bonnie had promised was two weeks; she hadn't seemed to be promising any miracle.

"You're blind," she snorted and decided to change the subject quickly. "So how long have you known Red and Anna?"

"Since I was a little boy. Red was my dad's friend and business partner. But my mother sold Dad's shares to Red right after Dad died," Clancy almost reached across the table to touch her hand, then decided not to take a chance.

Angel didn't answer, and turned her head back to the sunset and the water. What would they talk about for two whole weeks? They'd shared something special ten years ago and she'd never let go of those feelings, but how could two adults build even a temporary relationship on the past? And she had to admit that there hadn't been all that much to it. Clancy would drive to the creek and she'd wait, quivering inside and eager for his kisses, until he got there. Then he'd take her hand and they'd make love under the tree branches. Afterward they usually went skinny-dipping in the warm water, sometimes to return for another session of insatiable teenage sex, sometimes to dry off and go home . . . always by the back roads but never down Main Street, because someone might see him with her and report it all back to Melissa.

"Penny for your thoughts." He dug in the pocket of his slacks and put a shiny copper penny at her fingertips.

"Cost you more than that." She smiled. "You better eat hearty and get ready for the big golf match, because you're goin' to lose. And did you already buy wine? If not, get two bottles, because I really like good wine."

"I'll buy enough to fill the bathtub, my lady, if it makes you smile like that. Now tell me about Conrad Oil Enterprises again. There's not an oil well anywhere near that lonesome old pumper on your property." He tipped the glass of iced tea back and guzzled more than half of it before coming up for air.

"Everyone thought I was crazy as old Roy," she laughed. "Remember him. He used to walk up and down the streets in Tishomingo and he wore at least five watches on each wrist and blue plaid shorts."

"And a yellow checked sports coat and a big, wide tie with purple polka dots," he finished for her. "Gee, I hadn't thought about him in years. Remember how he used to hang around in front of the Armstrong Clothing Store? One day I asked him why he just stood there doing nothing, and be told me it was so everyone in town could see him. I didn't even crack a smile. I just nodded and went on."

"But he wasn't crazy enough to be put away." Her eyes sparkled in the candlelight. "Which is what Allie said about me. She was ready to throw me out in front of a semi on a four-lane highway and she was my best friend. She said that I could dig to China with a teaspoon and not find a tablespoon of corn oil, let alone crude. But I followed my hunch and it paid off. The president of the bank in Denison told me the only reason he was loaning me the money was because he'd always wanted a little place in the country, and when the bank foreclosed on my mortgage, he was buying it."

"Good Lord!" he exclaimed "You sure had a lot of adversity."

"Yep." She nodded.

The waiter brought their food and refilled their glasses, then disappeared again as Angel continued. "I was fresh out of college and no one offered me a job that I wanted, so I took my savings and hired a driller. That's how I started Conrad Oil. I could've gone to work for Red and Anna after that. Red said he'd pay big bucks for me to sit behind a desk and tell him when I had a hunch, but I wanted more than that. I wanted a business so all of my friends could work together . . . and I got it. The next year we incorporated Conrad Oil Enterprises. I hold the majority stake in the company and the girls all own shares, too," she said between bites. "This is good food. I told you I was hungry. I can eat like a fieldhand and I'm not one bit bashful about it," she added.

"Good," he nodded. "I like a woman who isn't afraid to chow down."

"What about you? Are you happy teaching? Funny, I always thought you'd go into the oil business somehow."

"Well, Red's been after me for a while to work for

him. Says I shouldn't waste my science degree. I thought about it, but I don't know. Teaching is fun. I like the kids and I like having summers off so I can fool around." He winked at her and Angel pretended she hadn't seen it. "I don't have to depend on a salary for my major income, thanks to the investments my dad left me. Say, do you want me to go to work for your competition?" he asked.

"Do whatever the hell you want to do," she said. "Right now, I just want you to finish eating so we can play golf and drink wine," she teased right back.

It was after eleven when they finished the second round of golf. True to her word, Angel won the first round. Clancy barely came out the victor of the second game, and he was prided himself on both his miniature and golf games. His ex-wife Melissa had hated both. She had never wanted to learn any game that took her outside where it was hot and she might chip a nail or break a sweat.

But it wasn't fair to compare Melissa and Angel. They were as different as two women could be.

He looked over at her. Angel seemed pleased with her win, but she was silent as they drove back to the motel.

Clancy parked the rental car in the spot marked with his room number, reached over the seat and picked up a brown bag. Angela smiled when she heard the tinkle of crystal glasses. Well, she'd whipped him at one round of golf, and if he was still as poor at drinking as he used to be, she might whip him at drinking, too.

"Wine on the beach," he said when he opened the

door for her. "Two glasses, one bottle. Half a glass and I'll be snoring, so there will be plenty for you," he explained as he took her hand and led her across the road to the sand, which glistened in the dark, even though there wasn't a moon.

He sat down on the sand and pulled her down beside him, then let go of her hand to take off his shoes and socks. He rolled up his khaki trousers haphazardly until they could go no further, just below his muscular thighs. "Got another one of those white thingy-jigs?" he tapped the plastic ring that held one side of her dress high. "Tie up the other side and take off those shoes and we'll go wading before we have a toast to the moonless night."

"I'm not afraid of getting my dress wet," Angel said.

"Oh, yeah?" Clancy scooped her up in his arms as if she weighed nothing and waded out into the ocean. "How much is it worth to you to keep it dry?" He pretended to almost let go of her.

"Clancy Morgan, if you drop me, I swear you're going to get wet, too. Don't forget that summer at the dam," she taunted right back.

"How could I forget that summer?" he nuzzled the inside of her neck, as he'd wanted to do all evening.

"Oh—" She pushed his face away, and flipped out of his arms. Just as she hit the water, she grabbed both of his legs and brought him down beside her, dousing both of them.

"You vixen," he blubbered when he surfaced in the knee-deep water.

"Don't threaten me if you don't want to get wet," she said sweetly, then sat down. "Being wet with clothes on isn't so bad. Now, I want you to sit beside me and tell me just exactly what is it you intend to prove or not prove in the next two weeks," she said bluntly.

"Prove?" He backed up until he was sitting in water so shallow he could feel the sand shifting under him every time the wavelets swelled in and ebbed back out. "What are you talking about?"

"I want to know why you're here. And why you're romancing me. I'm a grown woman now, and you might not like me when you get to know me this time. Do you just feel guilty about our baby? You never knew him, not even for the nine months he was mine. Don't feel like you've got to pay for your mistakes. You can't change the past and neither can I."

He reached across the wet sand to touch her hand. "Hey, I know that. But right now I'm trying to deal with feelings I didn't even really know I had. Ten years ago my hormones ruled my brain, and I was young and just plain stupid. Now, I guess I'm a little smarter. I want to get to know you again, Angel. And I'd want to know you even if we hadn't been together back then. You're one exciting woman."

"Thanks." She looked him in the eye, reassured that he wasn't shooting her some practiced line.

"I believe we have wine to celebrate our first evening together again." He lay back on the sandbar, reached as far back as he could, and grabbed the sack. "And wineglasses." He pulled out two cut crystal, stemmed glasses wrapped in white linen napkins. "One bottle of rare, vintage Asti from the vineyards of Italy, personally stomped just for us by purple-footed peasants."

She giggled and a thousand stars lit up in his soul. It didn't matter if there were dark clouds hanging low in the sky or that he didn't know a thing about Italian vineyards, his heart lightened just listening to her laugh. Maybe he'd send all her friends at Conrad Oil bouquets of roses tomorrow morning, just for giving him the chance to be near Angel again.

"To new beginnings." Clancy poured for both of them, handed her a wineglass by its slender stem, and clinked his glass to hers. He downed the mouthful of sparkling wine in one gulp.

She swished the wine around until its fragrance wafted up to her nose, then sipped it delicately. "Mmmm," she said. "Now I intend to enjoy every single little bubble, not send it down my throat like a shot."

"Well, that's the only way I can get it down. I still don't really like wine, or beer, or bourbon. I've never acquired a taste for any of it," he admitted honestly.

She tasted the sparkling wine again. "Suit yourself. But I think a glass of Asti on a sandbar on a moonless night is pure heaven."

Warm seawater sloshed up to her hips, billowing the skirt of her dress, and then the wavelet receded, leaving ripples in the sand in which they sat. Clancy watched the tiny sand crabs pop up and try to bury themselves again in the soft, wet muck before the next wavelet washed over them.

Oh, to be able to sit forever in such peacefulness, he thought. No meddling friends, no interference. Just blissful solitude as he watched her sip from the crystal wineglass he'd provided.

"Then are you going back to Oklahoma City to teach, or will you resign and work for Red?" She held the wineglass up to the faint light from the motel behind the dune, and admired the rising bubbles through the ornamental cuts in the crystal. "You never did say," she added.

"I don't know. But I can't keep Red dangling and feel right about it. I asked my mom for advice. She said to follow my heart just the way she's following hers and let the rest of the world be damned."

"Oh?" Angel finished her wine, and gently placed the crystal glass far enough away from the water's edge so it wouldn't be washed out. She gathered a handful of wet sand and let it slip through her fingers.

"She and Tom Lloyd are getting married today in San Antonio. They wanted it to be just the two of them for the wedding, but they plan on celebrating in style when we all get back."

"Tom Lloyd? You mean the—"

"Yep, Tom Lloyd. The maintenance supervisor at the cemetery. Seems she met him while she was out there tending to Dad's grave, and they got to talking. He lost his wife a while back and he was lonely, too."

"But—" Angel's voice held so much confusion he had to chuckle.

"I know," Clancy nodded. "Shocked me, too. Know what she told me? She said she didn't need money and she didn't care what her friends thought of him. Tom makes her feel special and Mama says everyone can get used to it or go to hell."

"Well, I'll be damned," she gasped.

He laughed. "You know, I thought she'd die a thousand times if I ever told her about you and the baby. Guess I was wrong about that, too!"

Angel sat still for a while, letting Clancy's news sink in. Tom Lloyd had taken care of the cemetery in Tishomingo seemingly forever. His wife had been her grandmother's friend, and had sometimes helped her clean houses when Granny got behind. Angel could remember thinking that Tom was the tallest man in the whole world when she was a little girl, and even when she finally reached her full height of five foot whatever, he *still* seemed like a kindly giant. He had never raised his voice and she remembered that he'd always kept his jet-black hair, which probably had gray streaks in it by now, combed straight back without a part. But he was still only the maintenance supervisor at the cemetery—and Clancy's mother Meredith was probably one of the richest women in all of Johnston County!

"I reckon there'll be talk in Tishomingo about that," she said finally.

"Yep, I imagine there will be." Clancy lay back on the sandbar to look up at the sky. Only when he looked up he didn't see the sky. He saw straight up the full, flowing skirt of a woman with long, thin legs, who was wearing black lace underwear.

"Hello, Clancy," a familiar voice said, and the soft feeling of contentment which had warmed his heart turned into a jagged edge of cold ice.

"Melissa. What are you doing here?" He jerked himself back up into a sitting position, well away from her.

"Who's your little friend?" Melissa said sarcastically.

Angel didn't turn around, but she did take her eyes off the distant horizon where the water and the dark sky met. *Of all the times for Clancy's ex to show up,* she thought bitterly.

"I said, what in the hell are you doing here?" Clancy asked again with a cutting edginess in his voice.

"Don't use profanity with me," Melissa replied prissily. He sighed. How on earth had she even known where he was? In less than a month she'd shown up on two sandbars just to torment him.

"Folks back home said you'd come down here for a little vacation, and I just thought you might like some company. Actually, I had a hunch that you'd come down here to drink in secret. If your little habit is getting out of control, I'd really like to help you. It breaks my heart to know that I can still make you so unhappy after all these years." She fidgeted with the silver bracelets on her wrist, sliding them up and down with a clatter that annoyed Angel no end. Melissa simpered at her. "But I see you've picked up a bottle to drown your sorrows, and a beach bunny. Aren't you going to introduce me?"

"Why?" Angel stood up, her soggy dress clinging to every luscious curve of her body and making Clancy work hard not to suck air just looking at her. "He shouldn't have to introduce us, Melissa. After all, you and I were in school together for thirteen years. I remember you very well. But maybe you don't remember me . . . I'm Angela Conrad."

Nine

"Of course I remember you," Melissa said in a sickeningly sweet voice. "You were the one who was screwing around with Clancy."

"I loved him when all you did was tease him. All you saw in Clancy was an easy meal ticket, and a handsome groom to stand beside you at your picture-perfect little wedding," Angela said in the same cloying tone of voice Melissa was using.

"Hey, Melissa. It's not as if I asked you to come down here. But I have a suggestion for you. Shut up." Clancy slowly got to his feet, dread filling his entire body. It was over now. Angel would fly home tomorrow morning and he'd never, ever see her again, and he couldn't blame her. She was her own woman now. She didn't need this kind of aggravation in her life.

"Of course you didn't ask me to come down here, darling." Melissa turned away from Angel as if it were beneath consideration. "But I figured you should be the first one to know some very special news. Our news. It'll change your mind about things."

"Don't tell me you flew all the way down here to tell me you're getting a divorce from Daniel," Clancy said disbelievingly. "Hey, I remember when you divorced me for him, and I didn't care any more by that point. What makes you think I'd care now?"

"Oh, hush," Melissa giggled, still ignoring Angel who was standing only a foot from her. "Did you know that Tishomingo is buzzing right now about your mother? Why, my mama is horrified that Meredith Morgan is marrying old Tom Lloyd. Here your dear daddy's only been gone four years and she's taken up with a man like that." Melissa was obviously trying to change the subject, but her smirky tone of voice hadn't changed.

"Melissa?" Clancy's voice had an almost threatening tone. "You still haven't told me how you found me here." Angel watched the scene between them, transfixed, as it were from one of those soap operas her granny had felt compelled to watch every day of the week.

Melissa pouted.

"Oh, all right. Meredith has my friend Christy house-sitting for her while she and Tom are off on their *honey-moon.*" She dragged out the last word as if she were a kid with a new dirty term that she was showing off in front of the whole playground. "Christy found a note that had the name of your motel and the phone number here in case of an emergency, and she told my mama. And I caught the next flight out, right behind you, to tell you the wonderful news I just mentioned."

"I don't give a damn if you bought me the winning ticket in the Texas lottery. You can have the zillion dollar jackpot all to yourself. Just so long as you leave me alone." Clancy picked up the bottle of Asti and the two wineglasses. "You're nothing but bad news, Melissa. So just trot back to the airport and catch the next flight home. Come on, Angel. I'll walk you to your door."

Melissa stomped her foot in the sand, practically falling off her high-heeled sandal when she did it. She put her hands on her waist and glared at him, as if a look could change the way he felt about her. It *had* worked—years ago. When she got this mad, he used to stop and listen, but something was different to-night. She felt as if she'd lost the control she'd had over him for all those years.

Angel glared at her. Damn the woman for having the nerve to follow Clancy down here! Damn it all to hell!

"See you later, Melissa," she said hatefully. "You, too, Clancy. I don't need a love triangle in my life." She picked up her sandals and started to walk away.

"Don't go," he said just above a whisper. "Please, don't go."

"Why not?" Melissa turned and lifted her shoulders like an offended female feline. "She might be rich now, but she'll always be white trash."

"Shut up, Melissa!" Clancy said furiously. "Don't you know it's over for us? Has been for years. Whether Angela stays or goes is her business, but nothing you can say would make me love *you* again . . . if I ever did."

Angel doubled up her fists, but she kept them down and fought the white-hot rage boiling up inside her. One good solid right hook and this useless woman would be sporting a crooked nose until she could see a plastic surgeon. Not that Angel wanted to fight her rival—tonight or ever. But she did have an urge to sock Melissa hard enough to send her about halfway to the horizon.

"Well, you'll love me when I tell you our good news," the heartless hussy went on. Angel fumed silently. "I do know you wanted to have a child when we were married and things just never seemed to work out. I'm real sorry about that. But now I'm pregnant, Clancy. And the baby is yours." Melissa's tone was unbearably smug, and her expression seemed to dare either of her listeners to doubt her announcement.

"You're *what?*" Clancy said incredulously.

"You heard me. Preg. Nant. *Pregnant.* Only by a couple of weeks, but you know how good these early tests are now. Must have happened that night at Pennington Creek when you were so drunk you didn't know what you were doing. Don't you remember-any of it, darling?" Melissa looked triumphantly at Angel and seemed to be expecting her to stomp away in a fit of anger, as she certainly would have done.

Angel stopped in her tracks, although she'd been ready to do just what Melissa had expected. That funny feeling she called "the hunch" came over her. It started down deep where the anger had come from just moments before.

She mentally picked up the pieces of this particular puzzle, and tried to put them together. It only took a split second to know something wasn't right and her intuition had never yet disappointed her. Angela had founded a multimillion dollar business based on it . . . and she'd be a fool to let this brazen bitch control her emotions or her life when she suddenly felt a hunch as strongly as she did now.

"You might be pregnant," Clancy shook his head in bewilderment, "but it's not mine and you know it. Nothing happened . . . except that you slapped me when I told you about the stillborn baby Angela had. That baby was mine. Now I might have had a few beers when you showed up again, but I remember when I've had sex, and I didn't."

" 'You were so drunk you wouldn't remember anything," Melissa smoothed the front of her skirt over her flat stomach. "I know you offered me bourbon . . . and then you called me Angel. Then I sat down on the sand beside you, and that's when you started kissing me, and one thing led to another."

Angela stifled a laugh. This would make Granny's soap operas as tame as a declawed house kitten. Melissa was lying, and Angela knew it as surely as she knew Clancy was telling the truth. So Melissa needed a husband. That meant the baby wasn't Daniel's or she would still be with him. Now wouldn't that set the old Tishomingo tongues to wagging? The social cream of the crop had gotten caught with her pantyhose down around her ankles.

"What are you laughing at Angela? You had your turn to have a baby with him. Now it's mine," Melissa sneered.

"Don't take that tone with me, Melissa. I'm not beneath you and I'm not the poorest kid in the classroom you used to pick on. I'm a grown woman who's smart enough to know when another woman is making a fool of herself. If you're pregnant . . . well, congratulations. When the baby's born, Clancy can go to the hospital for DNA testing." Angel moved over next to him and slipped her arm through his. "If it's Clancy's baby, then he'll be more than happy to write you a support check, but you know and I know it's not his. Get back in your car, wherever it is, and get the hell out of here. Because this beach ain't big enough for us both, and I'm staying."

Clancy didn't know whether to spit or go blind. He expected Angel to walk away from him and never look back, and he wouldn't have blamed her if she did. Lord, what in the world had happened in the middle of this argument to change her mind? Here she was plastered to his wet side as if she belonged there, and Melissa just stood in front of them with her mouth hanging open.

"Just remember, if I couldn't keep him, you don't have a chance," Melissa said. "He's never been faithful and never will be. I'm the only person in the whole world who ever understood him."

"Honey, you couldn't keep him because I had him first." Angel couldn't resist the barb. "Clancy, I do believe you said something about walking me to my door. Maybe you'd like to come in for a soda while I have another glass of this wonderful Italian wine. You know, I think a storm is rolling in tonight, Melissa. I hope you don't have trouble on your return flight. Come on, Clancy. These wet clothes are beginning to get sandy and I need a shower." She pulled him away.

"Clancy, if you walk away with that bitch, you'll never see this baby." Melissa raised her voice and Angel's flat-palmed slap answered her.

"Don't call me names," Angel ground out. "Clancy won't have to see this baby of yours, because when the tests come back, it won't be his. I'd be willing to stake Conrad Oil on it, Melissa, and you know I'm right, so go find some other sucker to pin your mistake on."

"Are you going to let Angel run your life, Clancy?" Melissa held her red cheek and let a few well-trained tears run down to her quivering jawbone.

"Like a toy train, if she'd do it for me," Clancy smiled for the first time since he'd flopped on his back and stared up his ex-wife's skirt.

"Then both of you can go straight to hell, and, Clancy, you can just wonder forever if this baby belongs to you." Melissa stomped silently through the sand and back to her car, where she slammed the door and peeled out, leaving the beach behind her as she squealed the tires on her rental car loudly enough to wake up half the residents of the motel.

Angel sat right back down in the water and poured herself another glass of wine. "And now, what have you got to say for yourself?"

Clancy's heart fell again. She would never believe that he had told the truth. She'd certainly never trust him again and they weren't even begun to renew their romance. In fact, they were back where they started and he was sure he'd never see the day when he'd take her to dinner again.

"This is what happened. I you at left the cemetery, stopped by the liquor store, got some beer and bourbon and decided I'd get drunk and give myself a hellacious headache. I wanted to hurt so much I couldn't think of you and I couldn't see that tombstone with my son's name on it. I wanted to forget what a heel I'd been to you, and a good old-fashioned hangover seemed like an appropriate punishment." Clancy sat down beside her.

The pieces were tumbling into place in her hunch factory again. Clancy was telling the truth. "I see. And where did you go to create this humongous headache?"

"To the dam. I took an old blanket and spread it out in our spot, and I sat down on the sandbar and put my feet in the water and started drinking beers. One minute I was all by myself. The next minute, Melissa was there beside me. Lord, at first I thought it was you . . . I guess I hoped it was you. She thought she'd ruined my life by divorcing me, so I just told her why I was getting drunk. She slapped my face and stormed off, saying if I didn't tell my mother, the whole story, she would the next day," Clancy said.

"And did you?" Angel held her breath.

"Yep, I did. Thought she was going to take a hickory switch to me even though I'm twenty-eight years old and survived marriage to that witch and then the divorce. Then she told me about Tom and I told her I realized what a big mistake I made all those years ago," he finished.

"Then your mother knows about me?" Angel could hardly believe her ears.

"She's the one who insisted I fly down here. She said to face the future I had to bury the past and learn to appreciate the present . . . or some philosophical thing like that. Seemed smart to me at the time. I sure never expected to look up and see Melissa on the beach tonight. Whatever possessed her to fly down here is a mystery to me, Angel."

Angel thought for a long moment. "So she and her husband Daniel are getting a divorce. It's scary, Clancy. She moved out of her parent's house into the dorms and a secure relationship with you, then into marriage with you, and then into marriage with him as soon as possible. Now she's about to lose her security blanket. But she doesn't care if it's a bit worn around the edges and tattered, it's better than nothing."

"Are you saying I'm nothing?" Clancy had to smile at her choice of metaphor.

"I'm explaining her actions," Angela said unruffled. "Melissa's scared to face life alone. At one time she could control you and it might have worked again, if I hadn't been there beside you. Her story didn't make sense. You won't even have a full glass of wine with me, but you'd get drunk with the woman who left you for another man? Come on, even you have a bit more class than that."

Clancy winced at the backhanded compliment. "Thanks, and I do mean it," he sighed. "I really did not have sex with her. I had drunk several beers and I was a little tipsy, but I did not touch her, and that's a promise. If she's pregnant, I'll go for DNA testing, I promise."

"Well, let's see," Angela said. "But for now I think I'd like to call it a day. I need a long, hot shower to wash all this sand out of my underwear, and you, sir, probably do, too. So you can walk me to my door. But I was only kidding about you coming into my room for a cold soda. I learned my lesson about sex many years ago. I don't fall into bed with a man just because he has lots of sex appeal and a nice smile."

"Thanks for the compliments." Clancy helped her up.

They walked up the sandbar in silence, each thinking about the evening's events. He knew the head of all the guardian angels in heaven had been working on his side tonight. Clancy felt a crazy need to drop down on his knees and give thanks even if he never knew just exactly what it was that had turned her around in the middle of that triangular argument.

She hadn't realized how much Clancy meant to her until the thought of Melissa snaring him with a lie shocked her into awareness. Angel might not be ready for a relationship with the man, but she'd be damned if she stood by and lost the best golfing partner she'd ever found. And, besides, she got the whole bottle of Asti when he was buying!

When they reached the top of the stairs, he unlocked her door for her, handed back the key and started to the next room. "Thanks. I mean it, Angel," he said over his shoulder.

"Is that all? I didn't say I wouldn't appreciate a nice warm kiss to finish off a wonderful day," Angel cocked her hip in that provocative pose that made his blood boil, and waited for one sweet second for him to turn back around to her.

Clancy gathered her slowly into his arms, realizing that this was the grand finale of the whole disastrous, wonderful day, and when his lips met hers, she opened hers slightly to taste the sweet smoothness of his part of a glass of wine still on his tongue. He never knew Asti could taste so good. Maybe he'd been drinking it all wrong all these years. He just needed to funnel it through Angel Conrad's sexy mouth to appreciate the full flavor.

They were both adults and they'd kissed other people in the past ten years. But when they closed their eyes and flesh finally met flesh again, it was as if the heavens opened and stardust glittered above them in the darkness of the night.

"Thank you again, my sweet Angel," he murmured softly into her neck, dreading the moment he would have to pull away and go to his lonely room.

"Oh, Clancy." Angel pushed him away with an honest, warm smile. "See you in the morning. I'll be on the balcony throwing toast to the turtles early, but you can sleep in if you've had too big a day," she teased as she slipped out of his arms and into her room, knowing full well how much she wanted to drag him in with her.

"I'll be waiting on my balcony right next door when you get up," Clancy challenged and he walked off to his own room, wishing he could have picked her up and carried her with him.

Ten

Angel crawled between the cool, white sheets, and stared at the ceiling for a minute or two before she drifted off. Suddenly the next morning the alarm went off and she didn't remember even setting the clock. She always woke early, read the paper and had coffee while she mentally went over the day's schedule. When she slapped at the clock on her bedside table and it rang again, she realized it was the telephone. "Damn that Clancy," she swore, glancing at the time and realizing it was only four o'clock in the morning. He'd probably stayed up all night just to beat her to the balcony this morning. Early meant seven o'clock to her . . . not the darkest hours before dawn.

"What?" she picked up the receiver and answered without opening her eyes all the way.

"Miss Conrad, this is the front desk. We're sorry to inform you that you'll have to leave within the next hour. We are evacuating the motel. The hurricane that was expected to hit the east coast has made a turn-around and is coming this way. Can I assist you in any way?"

"Good grief!" She was out of bed and on her feet. "What hurricane?"

"Blanche," he said, as if he were telling her the name of a hairdresser in town. "Hurricane Blanche. Been tracking her path all night, and the weather channel predicted she'd go to the other side of the state, but she made an abrupt about-face and headed this way with a full head of steam."

"Thank you," Angel managed to say before she hung up and threw a suitcase on the bed. She picked up the receiver again and dialed the airport. "I need a flight out of here to Dallas or Oklahoma City," she said.

"Sorry, ma'am. The flights that haven't been canceled are already full," the reservations clerk said, and Angela swore under her breath at the same time she heard an incessant pounding on her door. She jerked it open to find Clancy standing outside on the landing with his bags.

"I've called the airport and the car rental where I got the Cadillac. We can drive it to Oklahoma City and leave it there. Get in touch with your rental outfit car and we'll drop your car off on the way out," he said, picking up her suitcases and heading down the stairs.

"Wait a minute!" she called desperately. "What if I don't want to ride to Oklahoma with you?"

He chuckled. "You can go with me or we can ride out the hurricane on the beach. The motel is evacuating. I'll be back in two minutes, Angela. You don't have to get dressed. You look pretty cute in that nightshirt, and I'll drive, so you can sleep." He laughed again.

"Oh, hush!" She slammed the door, shucked her Betty Boop nightshirt and threw on a pair of shorts and a T-shirt, and dialed the rental company number on the keychain she'd pitched on the night table yesterday . . . Was it really just yesterday? A whole month's worth of staggering events had happened in a scant twenty-four hours and now some unexpected hurricane had decided to pay a visit. Did she have her girlfriends to thank for that, too? She tapped her fingers on the table and willed someone to answer the phone. Maybe the rental agency had been evacuated too!

"Thank you for calling Hertz," the rental clerk said cheerily. Was Florida full of crazy people who had no respect for hurricanes? And what did they do with tourists who needed a place to stay when the beach motels were evacuated?

"This is Angela Conrad. I need to return a rental since there appears to be a hurricane on the way," she said. "I just wanted to make sure someone was there this early in the morning."

"We're here twenty-four hours a day," the clerk said. "Park it in front and drop the keys in the front door slot. Angela Conrad, red Ford Taurus, credit back to your card? Do you need the address of a shelter where you can stay for the next couple of days until the hurricane blows over?"

"No, thanks. And please do credit it back to my card." Angela hopped on one foot while she put on a sneaker.

"Better hurry if you're planning on making a run for the border," the woman said. "Blanche is due in an hour or so."

"Will do." Angela crammed everything from the vanity in the bathroom in her last bag, quickly scanned the room, and was on the landing by the time Clancy started back up to help her.

They were thirty minutes inland, headed due north, when the wind and rain hit in a solid sheet, surrounding the car on all sides. Clancy eased up on the gas pedal and inched along the highway, gripping the steering wheel so tightly his knuckles were white. Visibility was two inches at most, with the wind beating a powerful, driving rain into the car in great waves.

"Maybe we should've built an ark last night," Angel whispered, awed by the force of the storm. This was worse than she had thought it would be.

"Maybe we should have found a shelter and not tried to outrun this," Clancy berated himself for putting her in danger. "I thought half an hour would give us enough time."

"Shhhh," she said "I don't want to spend time in a shelter full of strangers and homeless people. We'll get on the other side of the storm soon enough. Too bad we can't take part of it home . . . only without the wind. You know how much my gardener would like this amount of water in the middle of July," she said nervously as she watched a tree on the side of the road bend and sway, then disappear in the grayness. They could die in this stupid gray Cadillac out here in the middle of a gray hurricane throwing gray rain at them and no one would know for days. When rescue workers would come to clean up the rubble, there would be an overturned car, looking like a casket, with two bodies in it. What in the hell would the Tishomingo newspaper do with that story? Angel could just imagine the lead sentence. *Well-known local resident dies in crash with rich oil company president, formerly a local member of the white-trash sector, and former wife says she barely got out of the state before the storm hit!* Who knows, maybe the wrath of Melissa had caused the hurricane to take an abrupt turn. After all, she'd been a first-class witch for years. Maybe she had taken a correspondence course and expanded her powers. Angel visualized her in a long, flowing black robe, stirring a boiling pot full of liquid. She'd chant a while and then add a pile of frog toes and the powdered brain cells of a sea gull, along with a sprinkle of lizard liver, evoking the dark powers to bury Clancy and Angel together in a big automobile while Melissa laughed hysterically.

By eight A.M. they had crossed the state line into Alabama and traveled sixty miles in three hours. They hadn't seen or passed another vehicle since leaving the motel. Finally the rain lessened, making it possible at least to see the road signs from a few feet away, and her stomach grumbled loudly enough for Clancy to hear it.

"Hungry? I'm starving. Want to make a run for a McDonald's at the next exit?" he asked. "I'd do anything for a cup of coffee."

Angel sighed. "Me, too. Black and strong. And one of those biscuit things with eggs and ham and cheese, and a hash brown. Is it going to rain on us all the way home?"

Clancy grinned. "Probably." He eased the car off the exit ramp, noticed a McDonald's sign to the left, and after a quarter of a mile saw the familiar arches. "We're going to get soaked." He parked the car, amazed at how tense all his muscles were. "Unless you want to go to the drive-through window and eat in the car."

"Nope." She unbuckled her seat belt. "I'm going in. I've got to go to the restroom. Better to be wet with rain water than with what would happen if I don't find the ladies' room. Besides, I'm not sugar or salt and I won't melt. All that will happen is my curly hair will curl all the way to my split ends."

"Then let's make a run for it. Betcha I can beat you"

"Oh, yeah?" She grinned back at him. "On your mark, open the door, go!" And Angel splashed through the water, ignoring all the mud puddles and laughing all the way. When he reached the door, she was holding it open for him like a butler. "Come right in, Clancy Morgan. You just lost the race," she teased. "So you can buy breakfast. Besides, I left my purse in the car. I'll be sitting at that booth after I dry off with paper towels in the restroom." She pointed to the back, and left him standing in a puddle.

"Yes, ma'am," he called and went to order for them. By the time he had their breakfasts on a tray, Angel was sitting in the booth where she said she'd be. All her makeup was washed away, her shirt clung to every curve, and there wasn't a dry patch on her. She'd taken off her shoes and had them parked beside her, and every hair on her head was frizzed out. She was glad the management had turned off the air-conditioning because she shivered even without it.

"Breakfast is served, ma'am." Clancy set the tray between them. "Chow down. The lady at the register said it's a hundred miles to Montgomery and there's not a dry inch of ground between here and there, so we might make it by lunchtime if we're lucky."

"Ummmm." She tasted the coffee first, holding it in her mouth, enjoying the warmth and the flavor. "Want me to drive a while? How far is it by car to Dallas from Alabama, anyway?"

"Depends on where you start from, but we've got two weeks to get there, don't we?" he teased

"No." She bit into the biscuit. "I might keep company with you for two weeks in a resort, but not in a car. We can drive until we get there . . . straight through. You can sleep while I drive and I'll sleep while you drive. A day, two days?"

"Two if the rain stops. One night in a motel on the way," he guessed. "You're off work for two weeks, though. Let's take our time."

"I'm goin' home, Clancy," she declared as if that would make it final. "You can drop me in Denison on your way."

"Is your car at the airport?" he asked.

"Patty drove me to Dallas," she said between bites. "Oh, my Lord, I'd better call her. She'll think we both got blown away by Hurricane Blanche."

"My truck is at the airport in Oklahoma City, and this car can be left there. Why don't you come home with me for the rest of the vacation? How long has it been since you went back to Tishomingo? Mama would love to see you." He threw out the ideas that had been turning in his mind all morning as he'd battled the wind and rain to get them this far.

Angel practically choked on the hash brown patty. "Are you inviting me to go home with you? To Tishomingo—as a house guest in your mother's home?"

"Yes I am." He nodded "Or I'll get you a room at the only motel left in town for the rest of your vacation if you'd be more comfortable there. But we've got a guest house out by the pool. It's got two separate rooms with two outside entrances. Thought maybe you could stay in one and I'll stay in the other. That way Mom and Tom can have a little bit of privacy in the house. It is their honeymoon, remember?"

"Can I think about it for a while?" Her big green eyes were softer than he'd seen them since they were in high school. With the ringlets around her face, she looked more like one of those dark-haired angels in his mother's curio cabinet than she did a real live woman.

"Sure. I figure we might get in by tomorrow evening if the rain lets up. You can think about it until then." His heart skipped a beat because she hadn't definitely said no and demanded he take her to the airport in Montgomery to fly home from there.

Angel had left a message on Patty's answering machine telling her friend that she was in a world of trouble, that the hurricane hadn't blown her and Clancy away yet, and she'd call again in a couple of days. Then she ran back to the car in the driving rain and hopped into the backseat. By the time he opened the door to his side of the car, she was opening a suitcase, taking out clean underwear, a dry shirt and pair of shorts, and jerking her wet shirt over her head "Keep your eyes on the front window," she told him when he dove for the front seat. "I'm changing clothes back here and then I'm crawling over the seat. You can do the same when I'm finished. Unless you're too damned tall and old to crawl over the seat. Lord, it feels wonderful to wear dry clothes. I'm glad I brought these old sweat pants and shirt. They're soft and warm. I may sleep all the way to Oklahoma City in them."

"Why do I have to keep my eyes front and center? There's windows all around you in this vehicle," he reminded her as he dried his hair with a beach towel she threw over the seat.

"Anyone would have to press his nose to the window to see inside in all this rain. Then he'd have to break his neck to cop a peek at a woman who can dress faster than the speed of lightning." She wiggled into her dry things. "Now," she shimmied over the seat. "Your turn."

"You don't have to keep your eyes on the front." Clancy opened the door and quickly went from the front to the backseat where he opened his suitcase. "I don't mind one bit if you turn around and stare at me."

"I'll just look forward," she declared, but she didn't tell him she could see him from the chest up in the corner of the mirror.

He finished dressing, then crawled over the seat with as much agility as she had, amazing both himself and her at the same time. "I haven't been wet like that—"

"Since early last night, but it didn't feel the same then, did it?" She finished the sentence for him.

"That was voluntary." He grinned and started the car, and they drove for hours. Neither of them felt much like talking, until Angel spotted something.

"Look!" Angel pointed out his window, just missing his nose by an inch in her excitement to show him. "That's the most beautiful rainbow I've ever seen. The colors are so bright. Look at that purple, Clancy!"

"I can see it, Angel, honest. Want me to stop the car so it won't get away before you've looked your fill?" he grinned.

"No, but look at the blue. And I can see the whole arch. Do you think there's a pot of gold at the bottom?"

"You're the one with the hunch power, Angel. What do you think is at the bottom of the arch? A pot of gold or an oil well?" he teased.

"A motel with hot water and big, fluffy towels." She caught his light tone, glad the tension of the hurricane was finally over, but realizing in her heart she had a decision to make before the emotions surging in the center of her soul would calm down.

"Your wish is my command," he said as he pulled under the awning of the Holiday Inn. "One room or two?" he asked before he got out of the car.

Her heart screamed one and her mind screamed two just as loudly. "It doesn't matter. One if it's got two beds. Two if they've only got a bed in each. I'm not afraid of you, Clancy, but we're sleeping in separate beds tonight, and that's a fact."

"Whatever you want," he said, and went inside to ask the desk clerk for a room with two king-size beds.

"Got one left," the clerk said "And it's close to the restaurant and club, too. Serve a pretty mean surf-and-turf supper there, and a band plays on Friday and Saturday, but not tonight." He took Clancy's credit card and handed him a key.

"Dress for dinner," he said when he got back to the car. "But no dancing, since it's only Thursday night. However, if you'd like to stay over through tomorrow night, I'll take you back there and we can dance the soles right off your shoes."

"Oh, sure, and take until Saturday night to get to Tishomingo. No, thank you! Cooling my heels in a motel is not exactly what I had in mind for a vacation after all these years. But then a hurricane, a twenty-four-hour drive and kinky hair wasn't either. Show me to the room and let me have a shower before I turn into a raving lunatic," she teased.

"Then you are coming to Tishomingo with me?" Clancy asked incredulously, as he opened the door for her and then carried an armload of bags to the motel door she already had opened.

"Sure, I am." Angel smiled radiantly, her mind made up at last. "And in a week, you'll send me packing back to Denison with your blessings. You might even get a bottle of wine to celebrate your good fortune in getting rid of me! I get the first shower and the bed over there is mine." She pointed to the bed farthest from the door and closest to the bathroom.

"I'm honored," he said.

"That I get the first shower and the bed closest to the bathroom," she taunted.

"I mean that I'm honored that you're goin' home with me, you vixen," he laughed. "Go use up all the hot water and towels and put on something stunning so all the men in the restaurant will want to trade places with me tonight. Even if we can't dance forever, they'll be green with jealousy that they can't at least saunter over to our table and ask you for a waltz."

"Yes, sir." Angel snapped a salute and, attempted to click her bare feet together. She unzipped the biggest case, took out her makeup kit and white terry bathrobe and disappeared into the bathroom.

Clancy could hardly believe his good fortune. He was sure she would walk away from him last night at the beach when Melissa announced she was pregnant. Then he figured she'd throw a fit at even the mention of spending the rest of her long-deferred vacation in Tishomingo. Lord the town was so tiny there wasn't anything to do but a little golfing and fishing. There wasn't even a nice place for dinner and dancing, but the thought of going there seemed to brighten her eyes and perk her up more than anything he'd mentioned in the past twenty-four hours. Then it dawned on him why it was so important to her and a heaviness replaced his light mood. How could he have been so thoughtless all those years ago? Well, he wasn't a stupid scared kid any more and he'd show her just what she really was beginning to mean to him . . . right back where both their roots were!

Angel let the hot water soak through her tired muscles. She poured apple-scented shampoo into her hair and lathered it until she looked like an upside-down Santa Claus. After she rinsed it, she wrapped her head in a white hotel towel, dried off, and slipped on her white terry robe. "Good grief!" she exclaimed when she looked into the vanity mirror. "I've agreed to go home with him." The idea hit her as hard as Hurricane Blanche had just hit the Florida coast, and would probably do her as much damage.

"Hey!" Clancy yelled from outside the door. "Leave

me some hot water. Remember I have to shave. You don't want to go out with me looking like a grizzly bear," he said.

"Oh, hush." Angel opened the door to find him leaning against the jamb. "You do look like you need to shave." She touched his face and he almost jumped from the sensation. "I'll get dressed while you shower and find me a two-by-four."

"Why do you need a two-by-four?" He cocked his head to one side, and gave her a questioning look.

"To beat the women off of you." She shrugged. "Don't take all night. I'm starving. But weak as I am, I can knock out any woman in the place who thinks she can walk out with what's mine."

Clancy just grinned.

Eleven

"Clancy, we can't expect to go back in time just because you're taking me to Tishomingo," she said over a sirloin, cooked rare just the way she liked it.

"No, we can't," he agreed, cutting into his own steak, done medium well with just a faint strip of pink in the middle. "The last thing I want to do is go back in time. Lord, I wouldn't relive the past ten years for all the dirt in Texas and half the tea in China. Not unless I could go back with the full knowledge I have today and redo most of it, but that's not possible. I want to forget the past and enjoy the present—thanks

to you"—Clancy held up his tea glass in a toast—"and
have warm, fuzzy thoughts of the future. We've both
got heartaches we need to get over. And the place to
do it is in Tishomingo."

"You're pretty wise for a selfish son-of-a-bitch." She
smiled.

"And you're pretty smart." He smiled back.

It was still raining when they finished dinner, so they
made a hasty run back to their room. Even though
there was an awning between the room and the club,
the wind had picked up again and blew a fine mist
around them, curling the hair Angel had worked half-
an-hour to get straight, and leaving water marks on
Clancy's dark-blue silk shirt.

"Yuk." Angel looked at herself in the mirror. "Why
any woman on the face of this earth would pay to have
a permanent put in their hair is a mystery to me! Oh,
well, you're stuck with Shirley Temple until it quits
raining. Turn on the television, please. We get HBO
here. Maybe there's a movie we can watch. I hope it's
not *Waterworld*, though. Lord, I may never fuss about
summer droughts again!"

Clancy fluffed the pillows on his bed, carefully took
off his shoes and damp shirt, and lay back in comfort
before he pushed the button on the remote, turning
on the television. A news report showed the damage
done by Hurricane Blanche, who hadn't finished tear-
ing up the gulf coast of Florida just yet. A few seconds
of footage along the strip where they'd been just last
night flashed across the screen.

Angel wondered if it had just been a dream that
she'd lolled in the calm waters in her sundress and

drunk wine from a crystal goblet with Clancy. Maybe after a while someone would pinch her and she'd awaken in her bedroom at the farm and smell the aroma of bacon coming from the kitchen where Hilda rattled pots and pans, and Jimmy puttered around in the garden.

Clancy flipped through the channels until he found the one which scrolled the evenings offerings across the screen. *"Something to Talk About,* is coming on in ten minutes. It's a comedy with Julia Roberts," he said, as she dug through her suitcase in search of night-clothes.

"Sounds safe enough." Angel disappeared into the bathroom and came out in less than a minute, bare-foot and wearing the Betty Boop nightshirt. She hung her sundress on one of the hangers provided by the motel and pulled down the covers on her bed.

"You could sit next me for the movie," Clancy pat-ted the edge of the bed beside him. "We could pretend we were at the picture show. I think there's even one of those hurry-up bags of popcorn beside the micro-wave the table over there," he suggested.

"Nope, this is fine," Angel fluffed her pillows and got comfortable. "This better be a funny movie or I'll fall asleep." She couldn't remember the last time she'd watched a movie, could scarcely remember the last time she had two whole hours to do nothing. If Conrad Oil Enterprises didn't claim her hours, then the farm did.

"Oh!" she exclaimed, remembering a promise she'd made to herself. "I've got to call Patty before the movie starts and tell her that the guillotine that's going to chop off her head is only held up by a skinny hair." She dialed the familiar number and got the answering machine, which she talked to in a tone of voice she hated, but always used when talking to a silly machine.

"Patty, pick up the phone if you're there. You can only avoid me so long before you have to face the music. Okay, it all adds to the force of the blow." She smiled when she thought again of the power of the hurricane and her previous thoughts of Melissa doing a witchy watusi around a boiling cauldron. "We've survived another day and I'm going to Tishomingo for a while, but I'll be home soon. Remember, you are in trouble," Angel singsonged and then smiled sweetly at Clancy as she put the phone receiver back in the cradle.

"Movie time," he announced.

They laughed, she sighed, and he declared he would never eat her cooking when the movie was over, since Julia Roberts, who played the wife, had made the unfaithful husband sick by putting something in his food.

"You don't have to worry about it, Clancy. I don't cook," she said.

"But—" He was astounded She played golf. She shot a mean game of pool. She ran an oil company with the moxie of a man, and even Red stood in awe of her abilities.

"I don't. Really and truly. I do not cook," she said, unashamed. "Granny did the cooking when she was alive. And she did a fine job, I didn't need to know how. Then when she died, I learned I could live on cans of pork and beans and wieners from the grocery store. By the time I got tired of that menu, I was in the oil business. Hilda cooks for me, and she—"

"Threw me down on the porch on my face," he laughed.

"She did what?"

"I was asleep in the porch swing and she flipped it so I'd fall out on the porch. Said she wasn't tellin' me where you were goin', and I'd better get in my fancy car and get out of there."

"That Hilda." Angela shook her head. Damn it, had everyone been in on this since the first day?

"Sleepy?" Clancy asked. "Or ready for another movie? Looks like *Eraser* with Arnold is next in line."

"Leave it on if you want. I'll fall asleep in the middle of it I'm sure. Wake me early enough so I can enjoy a morning shower and brush my teeth." She cuddled down in the bed and shut her eyes.

"Good night, Angel," he whispered.

" 'Night, Clance," she mumbled, but didn't open her eyes.

He watched all of the movie, but he didn't remember much of it. All he could think about was his Angel, sleeping soundly beside him in the next bed. If he shut his eyes, he could see her looping her arm through his on the beach last night, and later, running through the mud puddles to hold open the McDonald's door for him. After another look at the news coverage on the beach, where it seemed Hurricane Blanche was tired of playing and decided to go back out in the ocean, he padded quietly to the bathroom to take a shower and brush his teeth.

When Clancy returned, he stood beside her bed for a full minute just watching her sleep peacefully, and wondered what it would be like to see her face the first thing every morning. On a whim, he bent down and lightly kissed her forehead.

"Clancy," she mumbled.

"Good night, my angel," he whispered softly in her ear.

Before he could raise up, she wrapped her arms around him and pulled his mouth down to hers for a searing kiss which opened her eyes and made him shudder.

"I told you . . ." She pulled away.

"Hey . . ." he backed up and put up his hands like the victim in an Old West bank robbery, "You started it I just stole one kiss on the forehead and said good night."

"Oh, I must have been dreaming," she remembered "We were . . . never mind." She looked bewildered. She had been dreaming they were on the banks of Pennington Creek again. But they weren't teenagers anymore and she was enjoying kisses just like the one she'd awakened to. "This is crazy, Clancy." She sat straight up and patted the bed beside her.

"Sorry I woke you, honey." He sat down and took her hand in his. She reached out to touch the soft hair on his chest where the silk bathrobe parted, and the thrill of it inched up and down his spine.

"Kiss me again. The way you did last night," she said, pulling her lips down to his.

"Angel, there's nothing I would like more than to kiss you until we're both breathless, but . . ."

She pulled his mouth down to hers and claimed what had been truly hers years ago.

"Angel . . ." His low voice was almost a growl and he nuzzled her neck.

"Crawl in here with me." She pulled the covers back and invited him into her bed. Tomorrow she might be sorry. But tonight she was going to make love with Clancy Morgan, and the devil could have tomorrow, because right now was more important. The future was a blur, the past was a mistake, but the present was theirs. And Angel wanted to feel his body next to hers as she had on those hot summer nights under that old blue blanket long ago.

He left his robe and matching shorts on the floor and she added her nightshirt to the pile, along with a pair of white cotton bikini underpants. There was no hurry—neither of them was eighteen years old and neither of them had to be home by midnight. They enjoyed long, exploring kisses until they were breathless. Clancy touched all the soft skin he remembered so well. His hands were back home when they caressed her body and she sighed aloud when she ran her fingers through his hair and pulled his face closer for more kisses.

"Now . . ." She begged him to make love to her.

"Yes," he nodded and they came together again, more than five hundred miles and ten years away from the banks of Pennington Creek where they'd met the first time.

Except that this time would be better, Clancy vowed silently. The experience of years had taught him a lot about loving women . . . and he intended for Angel to remember this night forever. And he was no longer an eager boy who thought too much of his own satisfaction. Now, his greatest pleasure would be to take his time, arouse her slowly, and teach her every sensual delight he knew.

But Angel didn't want to wait. And she wasn't about to just lie back and let everything happen in its own sweet time. She ran her hands over the hard, muscular contours of his body and down over his taut belly, and lower. She drew him toward her and into her, and

Clancy sucked in his breath and trembled, fighting for control.

She rocked against him, until his big hands gripped her hips and made her stop. Angel held still for a moment, and he reached up to hold her head and kiss her, hard.

Angel responded passionately, as his lips sought hers, again and again, almost bruising in their intensity. He caressed her breasts and teased her nipples, tender with arousal, until she arched against him, lost in erotic sensation.

Clancy started to move then, with deep thrusts that made her nearly wild with desire: His breath came in ragged gasps, faster and faster, until Angel cried out in climax and he moaned roughly, reaching his own release simultaneously. He collapsed over her for a fraction of a second, but rose up on his arms to keep from crushing her, and kissed her again and again until she opened her eyes, dreamy in the afterglow of love . . .

Afterward she curled up to sleep in his arms and he drew her close to his side, blissfully content. Now what was he going to do to keep her there forever? What did Angel want? If she had a fling with him for two weeks and then went back to her oil company without a backward look, it would be what he deserved

Angel awoke with a start when the alarm buzzed at seven o'clock. She was still in the crook of Clancy's arm, snuggled up beside him. Lord, what had she done? This was all her own doing. She'd wanted Clancy in her bed last night and she'd made the first overture. Before she could get anything sorted out, he opened his eyes, smiled, and kept staring at her . . . making little ripples travel up and down her spine.

"Good morning," he finally said when she didn't blink her green eyes, and he wondered if she was regretting last night's lovemaking.

She nodded slightly. "Will we get to Tishomingo tonight?" she asked.

Evidently she was going to avoid any mention of what they'd done between these sheets last night, he thought. "Well, this is Friday. We could give ourselves plenty of time, and get there Saturday night. Want to stop off in Shreveport and play on a gambling boat tonight, or go dancing?, '

"Let's go as far as Shreveport and rent a motel room with one bed," she said seriously.

Clancy's face lit up.

"Or we can stay right here," he suggested.

"Nope, I'm hungry," she declared, and pulled out of his embrace. "Anyway, you can't kiss me until I brush my teeth."

She threw the sheets back and padded to the vanity mirror, unashamed of her nakedness.

"You are beautiful," Clancy exclaimed, feeling heat rise from his toes to the top of his head. He grabbed his robe so she wouldn't see the arousing effect she had on him.

"Coffee," she muttered with her toothbrush still in her mouth. "I need at least a pot of black coffee to wake up. Let's load this stuff up and go eat breakfast. How far is it to Shreveport?"

"Too far," he chuckled.

Twelve

"Maybe this isn't a good idea," Angel's stomach had butterflies the size of buzzards flapping in her stomach. She hadn't been this nervous since the day she signed the final papers, to purchase the building for Conrad Oil from Red.

"Hey, it's all right, I promise." Clancy shut the door of his Bronco and went around to open her door and gather up a load of luggage. "My mother doesn't bite, you know. And besides, she and Tom are still honeymooners so they won't even know we're around most of the time."

"You should have called first. She can't say no now." Angel nervously tugged her red shorts down and smoothed the front of a matching sleeveless jacket.

"Clancy!" Meredith Morgan, immaculately groomed as always, met them at the front door. "And Angela? Is that really you looking so grown-up? Come in. Tom and I just got home this morning. We heard about the hurricane and figured you'd come back."

"See?" Clancy whispered to Angel. "We thought we'd move into the guest house out by the pool if that's all right," he said, as he walked in the front door and set the bags down to hug his mother. "Can't stay in Florida, and Angel's still got the better part of two weeks' vacation," he explained.

Angel looked around at the inside of the house. It

hadn't changed much in the past ten years. The only thing new was the pool and the guest house, which she could see through double glass sliding doors on the other side of the dining area.

"Hello." She stuck her hand out to Meredith when Clancy set the luggage down in the living room, and went back for the rest.

"Oh, don't you offer me that hand, girl. Come here and give me a hug. I'm so sorry to hear about your grandmother's passing." She wrapped her arms around Angel and patted her back sympathetically. "She was a fine woman and I really liked her. Now, tell me about the hurricane. I'm glad you got out in time We were worried."

"So were we," Angel said seriously. "I didn't know if Clancy was going to drive us out or paddle us out for a while there, but we finally reached dry ground. Are you sure this is all right? I can get a motel room," she asked honestly.

"Absolutely not," Meredith brushed away the idea with a flick of her hand. "That's what the guest house was built for. The pool isn't the ocean, but I bet the sun's just as hot here, and you won't have to worry about a hurricane. Really, we want you to stay here."

"Thanks." Angel nodded "Clancy, honey, show me where to go and I'll help you," she said when he came back in the house.

Meredith heard the endearment and raised one eyebrow at her son, who grinned sheepishly. He looked different. Same dark hair, same walk, same five o'clock shadow that his father had at this time of day, no sunburn; nothing new . . . except his eyes. They were full of life and sparkle. And if his Angel was the one who put the glow back in his eyes, then Meredith Morgan silently swore she'd sell shares in Hades to keep her around.

"This way." He nodded toward the doors about the same time Tom opened them from the outside.

"Merrie," he said, "those ferns have got to be watered every day, and we're going to have to plant more— Oh, hello, Clancy. Didn't know you were back home." He grinned. "Oh, my goodness! Angel Conrad! Come here and give me a hug, child Lord, it's been ten years, since I've seen you and you're still as beautiful as you ever were, maybe even more so."

"You're still a giant," she giggled, standing on her tiptoes to hug him even when he leaned forward.

"And you're still too short!" Tom laughed. "Are you stayin' a while with us?"

"I guess so. The hurricane sent us back home, and Clancy says there's room for me in the guest house."

"Room for you anywhere you want to hang your hat around here," Tom said. "Let me carry those bags for you. We've got dinner reservations at some place over in Ardmore. You two have to go with us." He skirted the pool and opened the west door of the guest cottage.

Meredith was behind him shaking her head violently so he couldn't see it, but Clancy and Angel could. Tonight was a special surprise and she didn't intend to share it, not even with her son and his true love.

"Thanks, Tom," Angel said. "But it's been a long day, and all I want is a hamburger from the Dairy Queen. Then I want to come back here and sit in one of those lounge chairs by the pool until the stars come out. Airplanes were meant to get a person from one end of this country to the other, not automobiles!"

"I heard that. Then I'll get on in the house and get ready to go, and you kids can fend for yourselves," he said. "And Angel, it's mighty good to have you back for a while. We missed you and your granny when you left."

"Thank you." She patted his arm as he went back to the main house.

"Not that I don't want you," Meredith whispered, "but this is a special evening I had planned for the two of us . . ."

"That's quite all right," Angel said.

"You are going to church with us in the morning aren't you? The service begins at eleven," she said.

"Sure." Clancy nodded "We'll be up and ready, Mama."

When Meredith was back in the main house and the doors were closed behind her, Clancy turned to Angel, wrapped her in his arms and kissed her passionately. They had arrived in Shreveport by midafternoon, spent a couple of hours in bed, ordered pizza in and hadn't left the room until this morning. Then he'd stopped several times, pulled off to the side of the road, and leaned over for more kisses just as passionate as this one. "Just to keep me going until we get home," he'd explained each time to make her giggle.

"See, I told you." He raised an eyebrow like his mother.

"Okay, you win." Angel said. *But that doesn't mean this whole experience is going to be one, big happy ending to our love story,* she thought.

An hour later Clancy held open the door of the local Dairy Queen for her, then chose a table for two right in the middle of the restaurant. While he went to the counter to order hamburgers, she remembered what she'd thought about on the beach. She expected to be impressed if he took her to the Dairy Queen on Main Street in Tishomingo, and here she was, but the sun was still hanging in the sky and the new courthouse across the street didn't tumble into a mound of rubble. The very event which would have made her swoon at the age of eighteen wasn't so big a deal after all at the age of twenty-eight!

"Hey, Clancy!" Jim Moore's voice could be heard booming from two tables over. "Where you been, man? We got up a fishing trip last night down on the river and caught a ton of suckers. Larry fried them on the riverbanks and brought the beer. You missed a good time."

"I was busy outrunning Hurricane Blanche." Clancy grinned at his old friend. "She tore up the hotel where we were staying in Florida."

"We?" Jim raised an eyebrow. "You and Melissa getting back together?"

"Hell, no!" Clancy exclaimed.

"Oh, hi, Clancy." Janie came through the side door and walked up beside her husband. "You didn't order for me, did you?" she asked. "You seen Melissa, Clancy?"

"Yep, and I don't ever want to see her again," he said "Come over here." He motioned to his friends. "Get your food and come sit with us," Clancy nodded toward the center of the room where Janie could see a dark-haired woman she didn't recognize.

"Sure," Jim said. "What do you want, Janie? Bacon cheeseburger with extra cheese?"

"Not with all those fat grams!" She slapped his arm. "Give me a chef salad and a diet Coke."

Angel smiled up at Clancy when he sat the tray down

in the middle of the table. "Oh, my. Two bacon cheese-burgers, two orders of tater tots with chili, and two chocolate malts. Tell you what, since you've provided our supper, I'll wash the dishes when we finish, just to show you I'm all for equality."

He threw back his head and laughed. "Does that mean you'll tote the paper to the trash can and put the tray on the shelf above it?"

"Yep, and don't take it lightly, sir. I don't offer to do dishes very often." Angel unwrapped her burger. "I love junk food," she declared, rolling her eyes toward heaven. "Beats cooking any day."

"Clancy, darlin', have you heard about Melissa?" Janie pulled up a chair and sat down without paying much attention to the woman with him. He'd brought a few dates around in the past, but they never came back a second time, and she knew in her heart that someday he and Melissa would get back together. Besides, whoever this woman was, she'd probably get mad and go home if Janie kept a running conversation going about Clancy's first wife. At least it had always worked that way in the past.

And if that didn't work, Janie could manage to get this woman to herself for a few minutes and fill her in on how much Clancy really loved his wife, and it was beginning to look like things could work out for them. Janie would blink innocently and tell this one, just as she'd told a few others, that she didn't want to see her get her feelings hurt, but Clancy would never love anyone but Melissa.

"I'd rather not talk about her." Clancy glared at Janie but she didn't look directly at him.

"Oh, sure you would." Janie shook the salt shaker

over her salad. "She and Daniel are getting a divorce, and now's the perfect time . . ."

All the blood in Angel's veins turned to ice water. The burger tasted like sawdust and she knew she'd gag if she tried to swallow the bite in her mouth. So much for Tishomingo and coming to terms with the past.

"Janie, you remember Angela Conrad," Clancy reached across the table and took Angel's hand. "We graduated together and she played for us at the alumni banquet, remember?"

Angel looked to her right into the coldest blue eyes she'd ever seen. If looks could kill she would be stretched out on the floor, ready for the undertaker to embalm her. Janie and Melissa had been inseparable in high school, she remembered. And evidently, their friendship was still thriving.

"Hello, Angela." Janie nodded without blinking, recognizing Angel at last. "What are you doing back here?"

"Visiting Clancy," Angel felt a twitch at the corners of her mouth but she suppressed an automatic, polite smile. "Hurricane Blanche ran us out of Florida so we came home for a few days." She picked up her hamburger and forced herself to eat a bite even though it was tasteless, determined not to let Janie know even for a second that she was rattled.

"I see." Janie turned back to Clancy and ignored Angel. "Melissa told me she was going to Florida to see you and that you two could might work things out," she said, as if Angel were just another piece of furniture. "Then she called and said she was flying back to Virginia to settle things there, so I thought—"

"Evidently you thought wrong," her husband Jim

interrupted. "It's good to see you, Angela. Where have you been keeping yourself all these years?"

"Oh, I live in Kemp part of the time, and in Denison the rest," Angel could tell he was honest in his efforts to cover up his wife's tactlessness.

"What are you doin'? Besides outrunnin' hurricanes and singin' with that band of yours." Jim picked up his chili dog and took a bite.

"She's the president of Conrad Oil Company," Clancy said. He couldn't believe Janie could be so rude.

"You're kiddin'." Jim's eyes were round as saucers. "You *that* Angel? Red talks about you all the time. Says you're smarter'n anybody in the business. Lord, I didn't know he was talkin' about Angela Conrad."

"Thank you," she said. "How do you know Red?" It looked like they were going to have a three-way conversation which Janie could report back to Melissa because the woman was ignoring all of them and picking at her salad as if she expected to find a cockroach hidden under the lettuce leaves.

"I've been workin' for him eight years now," Jim said "Lots of us commute together down to the offshore rigs. Out two weeks, home two weeks. Janie loves half of it." He grinned, anticipating his own joke. "The half I'm gone." He slapped his leg and laughed, but his laugh was filled with bitterness instead of humor.

"Oh, shut up," Janie said primly. "It's just I can't get anything done with him home twenty-four hours a day for two weeks, Clancy." She continued to ignore Angel. "He's always underfoot somehow."

Clancy had seen Janie in lots of snits. Matter of fact, he'd seen Janie in almost as many as he'd seen Melissa

in. The two friends were cut from the same cloth, and
the only difference was that Janie hadn't been brazen
enough to kick Jim out . . . not yet. Clancy had seen
her flirting at the reunion and wondered if their marriage was headed for trouble, but Jim hadn't offered
any information and he sure hadn't been about to
ask.

"Janie," he said in the tone he used when he was
lecturing a student, "let's get something straight right
now. Melissa and I are history. She's the one who
wanted a divorce so she could marry someone else,
but it's over between us. And I'm not interested in a
rematch. She needs to get on with her life."

"Oh, sure," Janie flared up at him. "Melissa told
me she was pregnant and going to Florida to tell you.
Evidently she found you there with Angela."

"It's not mine." Clancy's temper flared as hot as
hers. He hit the table with his fist, making the two trays
rattle and other people turn and look at them. Then
he laughed out loud until tears rolled down his face
and he had to wipe them away with a paper napkin.
"This is so damned funny," he hiccuped.

"Are you crazy?" Jim stopped eating and stared at
him.

"No, not at all. It's the rest of the world that's crazy.
You're crazy, Janie," Clancy stopped laughing and
leaned forward until his nose was just inches from
hers. "Melissa may be pregnant. That's her business.
It might be Daniel's. It might be a senior student
where she teaches. But it's her problem. Not mine. If
she told you I got her pregnant, then your best friend
lied to you. If the two of you hatched up this scheme
together, then you know I'm telling the truth."

"Well, it weren't for you," Janie spun around and

stared at Angela. "Clancy and Melissa might work things out. They belong together."

"Janie, why don't you shut up?" Jim asked softly. "This just ain't your business."

"Yes, it is." She turned on him. "Melissa's been my best friend since we were three years old. So she made a big mistake by leaving Clancy for Daniel. So she got pregnant and her husband's not the father—but—"

"But who is?" Angela asked suddenly. So her gut feeling had been right. Clancy was innocent just as he said he was.

"Oh, go to hell. You never did belong to our crowd and you won't now, just because he's got blinders on," Janie hissed. "Don't think we'll all welcome you with open arms just because you slept your way to the top of some oil company and Clancy thinks you're hot stuff."

"Who's the father, Janie?" Jim asked, suddenly interested in the story. "Clancy says it's none of his doing and I believe him. I damned sure wouldn't be fool enough to remarry her. You treat me like Melissa's treated him and I'll boot your backside out the door, woman."

Angel's burger suddenly tasted wonderful. Janie was entitled to her own opinion. It didn't even matter that the woman had been rude. What mattered was that once again Angel's hunch had been right, and she hadn't let her emotions lead her down the wrong road. But Janie ought to know that it would be a snowy day in August before Angel turned her back again on the man she should have fought for ten years ago. If she had stood up and told Clancy Morgan right then that he was going to face his responsibilities and acknowledge their child, things might have turned out very differently. But she had been too insecure then. Now Angel Conrad was a force to be reckoned with, and she lacked neither security nor self-esteem.

"I'm goin' home," Janie stood up so fast she knocked her chair backward on the floor. "And you can either go with me, or sleep next to the river tonight with your buddies," she dared Jim.

"I'm finishin' this chili dog, Janie, and I don't doubt the riverbanks will be a pleasanter place to sleep than your bed. I'll be by the house and get my things tomorrow to go out for two weeks, and then you can keep things wonderful and clean." Jim didn't even look up at her.

"You're crazy, Jim," she said through clenched teeth.

"Maybe, but I still believe Clancy. And I can't believe even you would try to hogswaggle him into marryin' Melissa when it ain't his kid. What were you thinkin', Janie? That you and Melissa would laugh behind his back about it? I'm ashamed of you." He finally looked up at her, amazement in his face.

"Good-bye, Clancy and Jim. And Angela, you are a bitch," Janie whispered and stormed out the door toward her bright red car.

"Don't do it, Angel," Clancy's eyes were big as dollars. "I wouldn't blame you, but . . ."

Angel stood up slowly and followed her out the door. Clancy rolled his eyes and started to get up, too, but Jim put his hand on his friend's arm and held him down. "Don't. Let them alone. It's high time my wife found out she can't act like a horse's ass and get away with it. If Angela slaps her, then so be it."

"But . . ."

"Leave it alone, Clancy. Lord, who would ever have

thought Angela would run an oil company and do business with Red." He changed the subject. "If we'd been voting for least likely to succeed, she would have been right up there at the top of that list. And here she is. How'd you get hooked up with her anyway? Are things serious?"

"Hell, Jim, I don't know. I'd like for them to be. Uh-oh, she's just crawled right in the font seat with Janie—"

"I think we better straighten something out," Angel opened the door and sat down in the passenger seat just seconds before Janie started to back out.

"Get out of my car, you bitch!" Janie screamed at her. "Right now."

"I'm going to talk. and although you might not like it, you will listen," she said calmly, as if he was talking to a child. "Now, if you want to drive away, that's okay. Everyone in town can see you with me in the car with you, and you can explain that to Melissa when you talk to her again," Angel was as unruffled as a freshly made bed

"You're going to get out of my car or I'm going to throw you out," Janie threatened.

"Stop acting like a teenager. We're adults now, Janie. We're not in grade school and this is not a little red wagon you won't let me ride in. We're grown women. You're entitled to your opinion, and if you don't like me, that's fine."

"What?" Janie was bewildered

"I know your little friend Melissa tried to snag Clancy again, because she's desperate and needs a husband and he was always dependable. She just didn't figure on me being there when she arrived. There's no excuse for such a low-down, dirty trick, although you can be her friend and help her scheme if you want to. That's your prerogative." Angel looked the woman right in the eye, making her squirm. "Sometimes people don't like me, Janie, so I've learned not to care. Every day I make women and men angry, but I run a business. That's life in the real world. I made a big mistake ten years ago and didn't listen to my heart when it old me Clancy was bad news.

"I'm sure Melissa told you about my son. He was stillborn, and he looked so much like Clancy it broke my heart all over again to see him in that little blue casket. But that's mine and Clancy's business, not yours . . .

"I followed you out here to tell you two things. One, is you better not push that husband of yours too far. It's pretty clear that he's getting sick of it. The second thing is that you'd better never call me a bitch again— or I'll mop up the streets of this little town with you. I'm not from around here and I don't really care what people think anymore. Have a nice night, Janie, and when you go to sleep all alone tonight, remember it could be permanent!"

Angel opened the door and slammed it shut. Janie just sat there for a long time, thinking about what Angela Conrad had said. Whether she liked the woman or not, she made a lot of sense. Of course, she knew the truth about the baby. Melissa told her everything the night she'd gone to the creek to see Clancy. And she knew this baby Melissa was expecting didn't belong to Daniel, but to his best friend, and that's why Daniel had filed for divorce. Melissa wanted an abortion but she had already had three and was afraid to have another.

But to lose Jim? He wasn't the best-looking or the

best-built man in town, but he was faithful. And she had to admit he was a good man. But Janie seethed inside, wishing she could slap thunder out of that hateful Angela for being right. Perhaps Jim was getting tired of her attitude and was looking around. Goodness knows, he would have enough chances away in Louisiana, every other two weeks.

"No blood or broken bones, I hope." Clancy tried to smile when Angel sat back down and stuck the straw of her milkshake in her mouth.

"Nope." She smiled at him and Jim. "Neither one."

"Wouldn't blame you if there was," Jim muttered.

"I think she might want to talk to you. Go on out there. Betcha she's ready to tell you she's sorry," Angela said.

"Sure, when hell freezes over," Jim snorted, but he got up and left, evidently ready to take on his temperamental wife.

"Good food, Clancy. Thanks. Not such good company, but really good food," Angel said. "Hey, let's go to the creek where the old swinging bridge used to be and sit on the banks in the grass and see if any ducks float by. There used to be a few when I was a little girl. Granny cleaned a couple of houses over there and I was terrified of that bridge. I just knew the crazy thing was going to fall in the water and we'd both drown. I was probably the most excited person in the whole town when they tore it down and put in the new concrete bridge."

Clancy's attention was elsewhere.

"What'd you say to Janie?" he asked incredulously curiously. "They just drove off and Jim waved and winked at me. Angel, tell me what's going on."

"Not much. I told Janie a few things she needed to hear about Jim.

"And?"

"Oh, all right. I said that I didn't appreciate being called a bitch and I told her what I intended to do if she called me that again."

"And what would that be, you sweet little thing?"

"Let's just say that she seemed to get my point."

Clancy had to smile.

Thirteen

Angel and Clancy sat on the grassy edge of the creek, watching the big orange sun drift down behind the trees toward the west and the ducks floating in the current. She spoke first.

"You know, for years, I fantasized about the day you would take me to the Dairy Queen and we'd walk in looking like two people in love. I expected it to be the most wonderful day in the whole world."

He stroked her hair and wished desperately he had been able to make such a simple wish come true years ago. "I'm sorry," he whispered.

"Don't be sorry." She smiled brightly. "Tonight I realized that if we would have done things differently then, we wouldn't be the people we are today. What I feel for you today is much stronger than it was ten years ago, Clancy. If you had given up your hopes and dreams then, you might have resented me. I'm not totally sure we would have stayed together. You know, very few teenage marriages, especially those that start out with a pregnant girl, ever last.''

"Damn," he swore huskily, "you were wise beyond your years even then, Angel. And I'm really glad you still speak your mind.''

"Speaking of which, are we going to make love and then sleep in different bedrooms tonight? I'd feel really weird if your mother came to wake us up for church and we were in the same room.'' She looked at him without blinking and he thought he saw heaven inside her beautiful green eyes.

"Then we'll sleep in two rooms," he said "Want to go home and take a moonlight swim?''

"Sure.'' Angel was on her feet before he could move. "I need to work off the supper you fixed for us.'' She winked with the words.

A few minutes later, he knocked at the door to her bedroom in the guest house and waited for her to appear in that red swimsuit she'd worn on the beach in Florida. Instead, she opened the door just enough, took his hand and pulled him inside. Angel wore nothing but a barrette in her hair and a smile. Candles cast a soft glow on the room, decorated in shades of cool country blue, and the bed was turned down, waiting. She wrapped her arms around his neck and brought his mouth down to hers, where she teased his lips with her tongue as she ran her fingers through the hair on his chest. When he moaned, she pushed him toward the bed and fell with him, without breaking contact.

His hands massaged the soft skin he loved so much and then the sultry look in her eyes told him she was as ready as he was, and just as before, they were united on a plane that put soul to soul as much as flesh to flesh.

An hour later when Meredith and Tom arrived from their dinner date, they found them frolicking in the water as innocently as a pair of preschool kids. "Hey, you two, I thought you were tuckered out." Tom plopped down in a chaise longue and propped his feet up.

"Not me," Angel giggled. "I could swim forever. I've always loved the water." She splashed Clancy's face and then took a deep dive to the bottom where she swam until she reached the end of the pool.

"You cheated," he accused.

She shook her head. "All's fair in love and war."

"That's the gospel truth," Meredith sat down beside Tom in a matching lounging chair and reached across the space to take his hand. "We ate so much we felt like two little stuffed piglets and then I made Tom dance with me. He's not too bad." She smiled affectionately at him. "Surprised me to be swept around the floor in a perfect waltz. He told me in San Antone he couldn't dance at all."

Tom winked at Clancy. "Only stepped on her feet a few times."

"Ya'll still goin' to church with us?" Meredith asked. "Be up and around by eleven if you are. And we've got a bunch of folks coming from town for a poolside lunch afterward. Nothing too big. Sandwiches and a small wedding cake. The photographer will take a few pictures so we can show the grandchildren some-day . . . we hope." She looked at Clancy as if to remind him that the clock was ticking merrily away.

"We'll be up and around." Clancy nodded. "Maybe the photographer can shoot a few of me and Angel," he suggested, amazed that she didn't throw something at him.

Angel merely smiled demurely.

The next morning, Clancy arrived in the kitchen at ten o'clock, wiping sleep from his eyes and yawning. He wore a pair of his oldest shorts and a faded purple muscle shirt he usually used for fishing. "Mornin', Mama." He nodded at her and headed toward the coffeepot. "Tom up yet?"

"He's shaving," Meredith said. "And while I've got you alone I have a couple of things to say. First of all, you're a complete idiot if you let Angel get away from you this time. Lord, that girl is so much in love with you it's written all over her. Now, what's this about Janie insulting her yesterday? Did you take care of it?"

Clancy shook his head. "Didn't have to. Angel did. Do you really think she loves me?" he sipped the coffee and opened his eyes wide. "Hey, how did you know about Janie's snit?"

"Doesn't take the gossip line long to get hot. June called me this morning about the cake and said Janie told her mother she and Angel had . . . words. Clancy, this is a small town and you've got to be able to trace your ancestry all the way back to Noah before you're important around here. But I'm worried about Angel . . ."

"Hey, Mama," Clancy put his hand up. "I love her with all my heart. I just don't want to rush things. I'd marry her tomorrow, but I'm going to court her properly and then propose just like in the movies . . . on one knee with a big diamond in my pocket. Then if she wants a wedding big enough for Texas with all those women who were in her band standing beside her and a reception that lasts six days and nights, we'll have it. This time, my Angel is going to have everything I was too young and too insecure to offer her ten years ago."

"Don't forget stupid."

"Thanks a lot!" Clancy said indignantly.

Meredith grinned.

"Fine. I just wanted to know where we stood on this. Now get on out there and wake your fiancée up. She needs to munch a bagel or something before church. And if I hear anyone putting her down, they'd better be ready for a first-rate cat fight. She's the best damned thing that's happened to you in a long time."

"Don't I know it!" he exclaimed as he filled a coffee mug and carried it out the patio door toward her bedroom. He knocked gently at the door and waited, then knocked again. In a minute Angel opened the door, wiping her eyes with the back of her hand.

"Be careful, woman" he said roughly. "I'm carrying hot coffee. Don't be grabbing my arm and dragging me into your room for a wild, passionate love-a-thon right in front of my mother. She's watching out the back door. Besides, you wore me out last night."

"Oh, hush." A smile played at the corners of Angel's mouth and she reached out to take the mug from him. "Mmmm." She sipped the hot coffee and murmured appreciatively. "Leave the door open and come in while I wake up."

"Well, you've calmed down. Can't believe you're the same wanton hussy who threw me down on the bed and took advantage of me last night." Clancy sat down in a plaid recliner and kicked back while she crawled up in the middle of the bed and sat cross-legged, drinking coffee and opening her eyes by degrees.

"Mama said to come get a bagel. Real food will be served after church at a poolside lunch with some of the town folks coming for an informal reception. There'll be a wedding cake and a photographer for Tom and Mama. Think maybe you and I could have him take a few shots of us?"

"Why?" Angel woke all the way up. She knew there would be lots of familiar faces at the church, but she wouldn't have to make small talk with anyone for more than a few minutes after the services. Her mind went into overtime, thinking about what might happen at Tom and Meredith's wedding reception. Whether she liked it or not, she'd feel just as she did in high school. All those people would realize she was Angela Conrad, the poor little girl from the wrong side of the tracks, and they'd pity Clancy.

"Why not?" He shrugged. "We've never had pictures taken of us. The photographer's coming anyway, and besides, Mama and Tom would like one," he said.

"Sure," she said. "But you'd better let me have some time to get this hair under control if you want me to be ready for church and keep my smile pasted on for pictures, too."

Clancy stood up and bowed. "Your wish is my command. I'm outta here."

All four of them paraded into the church just moments before the morning services began. The minister, Dillon Williamson, had graduated just a year after Clancy and Angel, and this was his first year as a preacher in Tishomingo. He preached from Matthew 5, about the Sermon on the Mount, and Angela could almost feel the heat rising from the pews as he came to the part about judging one's neighbor. Then she realized that she'd done just that. She'd decided what people's attitude toward her would be before she even talked to them. It was pretty silly to think she would be the only one who'd changed by the time she'd come back to Tishomingo with Clancy.

Angel smoothed the skirt of her ecru linen suit and felt the security and warmth of Clancy's hand over hers as he reached across his lap and held her left hand with his and draped his right arm around her. Tom and Meredith sat beside them, only their shoulders touching, like a couple who had been married for twenty years instead of less than a week.

"Nice to meet you, Angel," the minister shook hands with her at the back of the church. "We hope Clancy brings you again real soon."

"Thank you," she smiled brightly. "Maybe he will."

The caterer had been busy while they were at church for an hour. Lace cloths covered round tables for four, arranged around the pool. Bouquets of fresh roses and daisies decorated the middle of each table, already set with silver wrapped in a crisp white linen napkin. Just outside the dining-room doors, a long table held barbecued brisket, chicken and ribs, baked beans and potato salad, along with several trays of fresh fruit, cheese, and raw vegetables. The three-tiered wedding cake, topped with a pair of porcelain love birds sitting in an orange blossom nest, was the centerpiece for the longest table, with a silver coffee service on one end and a silver punch bowl on the other.

"Just a little informal lunch?" Angel raised an eyebrow at Clancy when they walked out the patio door. "Lord, I ought to run in my room and put on the only party dress I brought along. I didn't think I'd be needing anything formal at the beach. Or Tishomingo."

"You look fine." Clancy checked her out, from her high-heeled sandals, to her shapely legs and then on up to the light brown silk dress suit, to the plain gold chain around her neck. Then he slowly made his eyes leave the place between her breasts which he would've liked to kiss right then, and go up to her face. Softly rounded, with a full mouth and flawless skin, flashing green eyes full of mischief, and to the top of that thick, curly hair, which she fussed and fumed about and he thought was adorable.

"I'd say you'd probably look good in a burlap sack tied up in the middle with a piece of rope," he said seriously, but his twinkling eyes gave him away and she slapped his arm.

"Oh, hush, what do you know?" she said, but her heart was happy.

"I know a beautiful woman when I see one," Clancy said honestly, taking her in his arms for a long kiss in spite of the catering crew around them. "Whew, I thought I was going to die before I could get another kiss." He wiped his brow dramatically.

"Clancy, you are full of bull—"

He put his fingers over her mouth. "Here comes Wilma Jones. If she hears you say that entire word, she'll drop down on her knees and commence to praying for your soul right here and now," he whispered in mock seriousness, then turned abruptly. "Oh, hello, Mrs. Jones. Would you remember Angela Conrad? She lived here when we were in high school,"

Clancy said, bringing Angel to stand beside him with his arm around her shoulder.

"Nope, can't say as I do." Mrs. Jones shook her head. "Pretty woman, though, Clancy. If you had half a brain, you'd keep her close to you. Now, where is your mother? I want to offer my congratulations. Some folks is talking about her marryin' up with Tom, but they're just jealous because they don't have someone treat them that good." The old woman shook her finger under his nose as if she were preaching him a sermon.

"Whew, close call," Angel giggled when she was out of hearing distance. "I think I like Mrs. Jones. She says what she thinks."

"Yep, she does. Don't you remember her from church when we were in school?"

"Clancy, I didn't go to this church. I went with my granny to the Methodist church over on the other side of town," she reminded him.

In a few minutes, most of the people Meredith had invited were milling around among the tables, visiting as they drank punch. Several stopped by to be introduced to Angel. Some remembered her vaguely; others didn't. But in a while, she began to feel more comfortable. Then Tom and Meredith appeared together at the back door and Tom clapped his hands three times to get everyone's attention.

"Merrie and I want to thank you for coming to share this special time with us," he smiled brightly. "We're truly glad you are here. I know you're all hungry and we appreciate you waitin' while the photographer snapped a few pictures of us. He's got a real strong camera. My ugly mug didn't even break it! Now, let's all form a line right here and start eating." He took Meredith's hand in his and led her to the food table.

"Clancy!" his mother called to him across the pool. "The photographer is waiting for you and Angel inside. I told him to be sure to take your picture together before he leaves." She pointed through the glass doors.

Clancy looked at Angel somewhat hesitantly. No matter what, he didn't want to pressure her. Angel nodded her assent.

"Let me freshen my makeup and lipstick. I'll just be a minute."

She passed Clancy's old bedroom and heard women talking. She started on past the door which was cracked just enough for her to see three women sitting on a bed, when she heard her name.

"Well, Janie told me that Melissa was pregnant," one of the trio said. "And it's not her husband's baby. She went down to Florida to try to get Clancy to marry her again, but she found Angel down there with him. I hope his mother knows what Clancy is getting into."

"Oh, Meredith's got her head so far up in the clouds, she wouldn't know straight up from backwards right now," the second one said.

"Well, don't knock it!" the third woman added tartly. "I've lived alone ever since my Frank died, and I don't like it. If I'd known Tom Lloyd was lookin' for a wife, I would've been out at that cemetery so fast it would make you swoon, Linda. Meredith is a good woman and she was a good wife to that first husband of hers. He was rich as Midas, too. But uppity. Can you imagine the late Mr. Morgan out there on his knees doin' yard work or lookin' at Meredith like she was a queen? Lord, I'd lay down on the freeway and die a happy woman for just one day of a good man lookin' at me like that."

"Don't change the subject. Do you really think Melissa and Clancy are through?" The first voice sounded incredulous.

"Of course they are! They shouldn't ever have gotten married in the first place. Melissa's always been hateful. But I don't remember this Angela much. I think she was one of those kids who blend with the background in high school, but she sure doesn't now. I'd love to have that figure she's got," the lady said and Angel almost giggled out loud.

"In my opinion Melissa has gone too far," one of them said. "I heard her husband's thrown her out. This is one time that spoiled brat isn't getting her way. But we'd better get on out to the reception before the food's all gone. Those women with husbands should be through the line now and us old widow women can have what's left." She stood up and Angel barely had time to ease the bathroom door shut before they paraded down the hall and out the door.

She checked the mirror and was only slightly surprised to see two round spots of color on her cheeks. It had been a long time since anyone or anything made her blush. She reapplied her lipstick and went back to the living room where Clancy waited patiently.

"Well, this will be a pleasure." The photographer eyed her, impressed with what he saw. "Don't often get the opportunity to look at someone this pretty through the lens."

She blushed again, and Clancy laughed. "Is that a touch of red I see on the cheeks of this brazen hussy," he whispered so low only she could hear him. "The same one who—"

"Shhhhh," she hissed, and spoke to the photographer.

"Thank you. Now where do you want us to stand?"

"How about here by the fireplace? Clancy, stand behind her and put your arms around her waist. Lean back just slightly, Angel," the man said, posing them with authority, "tilt your head just a little. Now look at me with those big, green eyes and don't smile," he said, and she smiled beautifully.

"Works every time." His flash lit up the whole room.

"Now let's do one in the antique chair. Sit down, Angel. Clancy, you stand behind her with your hands on her shoulders."—He demonstrated—"Like that. Very good."

In fifteen minutes, they were finished and back outside just in time to follow the three talkative women through the food line. Angel piled her plate as high as Clancy did, vowing she could eat a whole cow if someone would knock the horns off and heat it up on a charcoal grill for her. She even whispered in his ear that she'd worked up an appetite the night before, and then it was Clancy's turn to blush.

"Oh, that's Angela Conrad. She was Clancy's high school sweetheart before he and Melissa got married," they overheard one man telling another as they walked past.

"Well, when he gets tired of her, he can send her over my way," another one said with a chuckle.

"Oh, Raymond, you're too damned old to know what to do with her," the man beside him chided. "Besides, what would someone that pretty want with an old coot like you? I heard tell she's got an oil company and enough money to buy this whole town and plow it under for a garden if she wanted to."

"Gossip, gossip." Clancy rolled his eyes as they sat down at one of the tables.

"But it's nice gossip." Angel picked up a napkin and spread it out over her lap, then reached across the table for another one to set beside her plate. "I'm messy when I eat ribs," she said, "but I love them!"

"You love any food!" He laughed.

"You would, too, if you'd lived for a whole year on pork and beans and wienies," she said haughtily. "Besides, I'm one of those fortunate women who can eat whatever she wants and not worry about calories or fat grams. I'm so active and burn them so fast, I can eat what I want. And I love to eat . . . so I'm goin' to!"

"Yes, ma'am." He picked up a rib and bit into it, grinning at her.

"Let me have your attention." Tom tapped the edge of his glass with his fork. "The caterers are bringing a little champagne toast around to your tables now," he said, as women dressed in white slacks and tops brought silver trays with fluted crystal glasses of champagne and set one beside each person. "I would like to propose a toast to my new bride." He raised his own glass high in the hot afternoon breeze. "To my Merrie, who has made me happy at a time in my life when I thought happiness was just a dream I had lost forever. May we celebrate our fiftieth anniversary together," Tom winked at Meredith and clinked his glass against hers. "I love you," he said, as he looked into her eyes, not caring who heard him.

"Now, don't swallow it all in one gulp, I've got another toast," he said hurriedly. "This is to my wife's son, Clancy and his Angel. They were high school sweethearts, and now they're back together again. To you two kids. May you find the same happiness Merrie and I have found." He raised his glass high toward them and then polished off the rest of what was in it.

"Thank you." Clancy rose to his feet. "And a toast from me if anyone has anything left in their glasses. If not, raise your hand, and the caterers will be around to fill it again. To my Mama, who's been my friend as well as my parent. I thought my father was the most wonderful man in the whole world, and I have to admit, I didn't think I'd ever like anyone else taking his place. But Tom has made a place of his own, both in Mama's heart and in mine. So to Tom, my new friend. And to Angel—my one and only." Clancy clinked his glass with Angel's and tossed back the champagne in one swallow.

He had barely sat back down when one of the caterers brought him a cordless phone. "For you, sir. The phone rang in the kitchen area and one of my helpers answered it. The caller asked for you," he explained, and disappeared.

"Hello?" Clancy pushed the button and waited.

His eyes suddenly filled with tears and his chin quivered. "We'll be there in an hour and a half," he said. "Yes, she's with me. I'll bring her, too. Tell him we're on our way."

Angel looked at him with questions in her eyes. He'd gone from carefree and happy to looking just like he had that afternoon when he'd met her at the cemetery. The world seemed to be weighing on his broad shoulders, and there was no way out from under.

"What's wrong?" she asked.

"That was Anna. Red's had a heart attack. They've got him in the hospital in Denison and he's asking for the two of us. I was wondering why they weren't here."

Tears started down her cheeks, streaking her

makeup and landing on the linen suit in great drops. "I'll get my things together, Clancy," she said quietly. "We can leave in five minutes. And take a suitcase. We'll stay at my apartment in Denison. There's no need for you to come back here until Red's condition is stable."

Fourteen

Red's wife met them at the hospital door. Angel had never seen her look so upset. Anna's makeup was smeared from tears and her gray hair was uncombed. And the skintight jeans which were her trademark had long since lost their perfect crease from top to bottom.

"How is he?" Angel hugged her old friend tightly and felt Anna's thin shoulders shudder as she gave way to a whole new set of sobs.

"Red's goin' to make it. The doctor's said this heart attack was just a little one, but it sure scared me. While we were waiting for the ambulance, I realized that I didn't even know how much I loved him until I nearly lost him. I thought he was gone, Angel. I really thought he was gone," she cried on Angel's shoulder. "Oh, Clancy," Anna broke one arm away and brought him into the hug. "He started asking for you a couple of hours ago. I told him to wait till mornin', but Red said to call you right now. Only immediate family is allowed in intensive care, but he's pitched such a fit, they said you two could go in if it will calm him down."

"Are you sure?" Angel drew back and looked at her. "We don't want to upset or worry him. Most of all, we don't want to excite him. Maybe we ought to wait till tomorrow morning."

"Nope. Red intends to see Clancy tonight," Anna said. "I'll go with you up to the floor where he is, and wait in the lobby until he visits with you. The nurses damned sure would never allow all three of us in there at once. They said you could only stay five minutes. He's done told me what he intends to say, and I agree with him, Clancy. So listen to him. And besides, he's afraid to go to sleep before he speaks his mind."

They found Red in a quiet room at the end of the intensive care ward. An oxygen tube was stretched around his freckled face and attached under his nose. An IV dripped into his sinewy left arm, which had seen more hard work in its sixty years than most men saw in one lifetime. A green line wiggled across a television monitor to their right, recording his heartbeat and keeping track of everything going on inside that part of Red few people knew. He looked so much smaller in a hospital bed than he did when Angel had wheeled and dealed with him over oil wells. When he sat across a conference table from her, haggling over the price of a well, he seemed to be ten feet tall and made of steel. Tonight he looked like someone's grandpa, with wispy red hair turning gray, and deep wrinkles around his mouth.

"Afternoon, you two kids." Red smiled brightly at them, a little color returning and his eyes regaining a bit of their normal sparkle. "Glad you come down here. Saves me a trip up to your place, because I was determined to see you even if it hare-lipped the governor."

"Red, you old devil." Clancy bent over the bed and hugged him gently, then Angel did the same. "You've given us a scare. Angel cried all the way down here, and I couldn't swallow the lump in my throat."

"Good, "Red said. "I'm glad y'all love me that much. It'll make what I've got to say a lot easier. Now I've been asking—even begging—you to come to work for me, Clancy. You've always been like a son to me and Anna—the son we couldn't have."

The older man paused dramatically for effect and continued.

"Not that you've been around much lately. But you're a grown man with your own life to live and maybe you liked teaching high school kids. But the time has come for me to ask you a kind of a favor. Clancy, I'm too old for the stress of running an oil company. I've got to slow down."

"All right," Clancy nodded. I was going to call you next week with my decision anyway—"

Red held up a hand.

"Now hear me out. I'm talking about more than just a job. I figure I've got a few years left, and anything I can't teach you, Angel can. She's smarter'n me, anyway, but I'm older and I've got more experience, so you're goin' to learn from me first. Me and Anna had our wills drawn up a while back, and Texanna Red will be yours when I'm gone. All of it, lock, stock, rigs, and barrel.

"And the time has come for you to start learnin' how to run it. You're throwing away that degree in geology and chemistry, as far as I'm concerned.

"Now Patty told me last week about you two. You and Angel can be competitors or you can be partners. I don't give a damn if later on down the road you consolidate Texanna Red and Conrad Oil or if you keep them separate and fight over who makes the most money. And I want you to know how to run the company so I won't cash in the chips worryin' about some smart woman like Angel takin' advantage of your stupidity. And I'd like to see my two favorite people together before I die." He shut his eyes and breathed deeply, putting on a touch of a show but convinced that neither Clancy or Angel could figure that out.

"Red, I'll work for you, and you don't have to leave the oil company to me," Clancy almost blushed again.

"Get on out of here," Red whispered dramatically. "Come see me tomorrow. First I have to teach you to run it. Half of the company is yours right now, the rest when I'm gone. Maybe before that day, I'll get to bounce a grandbaby on my shaky old knees?"

Angel suppressed a chuckle. "Red, you connivin' old cuss, you're not about to run my life, even if you did have a heart attack. You might have grandchildren someday . . . but it won't be because you pretended to be sicker than you really were. You're tougher than shoe leather and buzzard bait combined. I'm goin' home and when we get back tomorrow, you better be sittin' up in bed, unwired from all these contraptions, and makin' oil deals on the phone. Good night, you old sweetheart." She kissed him on the cheek.

Red opened one eye to see her leave, then popped the other one open and winked at Clancy. "I'm holdin' you to your word. Call that school and tell them you're resignin' before school starts up and be ready to go to work in your new office on Wednesday.

That'll give you two days to catch that filly out there in the hall."

"It's not that easy, Red," he shook his head. "I'm not entirely sure she wants to be caught."

"Then you'd better hurry up, son, she's gettin' away." Red talked out of the side of his mouth and closed his eyes again.

They swung open the doors into a waiting room on the ward and Anna stood up, ready to go back to Red's side. "Did he talk to you?" she asked.

"Yes, Anna, I'll start at Texanna on Wednesday morning." Clancy hugged her again. "Tell him not to worry. If I've got a question, and I'm sure I will have, I'll just call Angel."

"Thank the Lord," Anna shuddered "I've been around the oil business all our married life. More than forty years, and I don't know jack squat about any of it. I can throw a party, flutter my eyes and help talk a deal, but if I had to fill out a single form, I'd probably be signin' the whole business over to a swindler. I'm glad you'll be there, Clancy."

He stopped dead in his tracks. "I forgot to ask Red where the office is located now. Is the company still based in New Orleans?"

"Hell, no!" Anna laughed. "We sold that building last week and moved to Sherman, Texas. Everybody on Red's staff is as happy as hogs in a big, wet mud puddle to be back. Not a one of them liked Louisiana."

"Okay, I'll call for the address," Clancy smiled. "See you and Red in the mornin' right here. How long do you think they'll keep him?"

"Couple of days, the doctor says—if Red promises not to go to work for two weeks when he gets out. And don't forget to call your mother and tell her Red's okay. Today was a special day for her and Tom—I'm so sorry we interrupted it."

Clancy stopped at the grocery store on the way home so Angel could pick up necessities . . . milk, bread, cheese, sandwich makings, canned soup, and fresh fruit. Then he followed her directions as they drove through town to her apartment, a two-bedroom condo in a beautifully landscaped complex.

"Welcome to my adobe hacienda." Angel opened the front door and stepped inside. She set the bags of groceries on the dining-room table and opened glass doors that led onto a private patio and a lush green lawn that looked like a little bit of paradise, right there in northern Texas at the end of July. "Come look here, Clancy!" she yelled across the living room. "Look at those big black storm clouds over there. We're goin' to get rain, right in the middle of the hottest part of summer."

Clancy walked up behind her and circled her waist with his arms, knowing a moment of pure contentment. "Guess hurricanes follow us wherever we go." He nuzzled her neck, enjoying the intriguing scent of her perfume.

"Oh, no, we don't get hurricanes here. We get tornadoes. And we're not havin' one today. The emotional roller coaster we've been on for the past week is enough to wreck my nerves. So I command that cloud, if it's planning to produce a tornado, to go tear up something a hundred miles away from me and you." She pointed toward the dark masses like one of Salem's best witches.

"I guess I better call the superintendent of schools tomorrow morning." Clancy changed the subject when he thought about all he had to do in the next few days.

"Yep." Angel nodded. "And I'm goin' back to Conrad Oil tomorrow morning for some peace and quiet. My vacation is over. But this whole week has been—"

"Wonderful," he finished for her. 'I'm starving, though. I think I got one bite of ribs before Anna called. And you didn't have much more than that. So, do you cook or do I?"

"I told you I don't cook. I can make a mean ham sandwich, and I know how to heat up a can of bean with bacon soup to go with it, but if you want cooked food, you'll have to do it." She turned and laid her face on his chest.

"Then it's ham," Clancy massaged the tension out of her shoulders. "I can't cook, either."

"Hey." She smiled "I understand. Tomorrow night we'll go to the farm and Hilda will feed us right. She might not even throw you out on the porch on your face if you're nice to me. And maybe she won't put rat poison in your potatoes. You've got two hours to stop that wonderful massaging on my back." She wiggled in appreciation.

"We'll really be starved in two hours," he reminded her. "Now, are you making the entree of ham à la sandwich? If so, I'll make the side dish of soup à la bean with bacon."

"Deal." Angel reached into the first grocery bag, pulled out a loaf of whole grain bread and a package of cured ham. "Let the gourmet cookin' begin." She started unloading items onto the bar separating the dining room from the kitchen.

"Why in the world do you live in two places?" Clancy opened the can of soup and rummaged around in the cabinets until he found a saucepan.

"Because I wanted two places. Sometimes I didn't feel like driving to the farm when we got home from a gig. Sometimes one of the girls needed a place to sleep if they didn't want to go home. So I rent this and own the farm. Okay with you?" She said testily.

"Fine with me," he laughed "It's a lovely condo, Angel. Got your special touches everywhere, just like the farm. I'm surprised you don't have a porch swing here."

"I've got one ordered. It's a wooden thing made to look like a miniature love bench," she admitted.

After they'd eaten supper and cleaned up the kitchen together, she declared she was changing into something more comfortable than the suit she'd worn to his mother's wedding party and disappeared into the bedroom. In a few minutes, she came back out wearing her Betty Boop nightshirt and carrying a quilted throw. She told him it was his turn to get out of his Sunday best and to find something he could lounge in while they curled up together on the couch to watch a movie.

"Angel, what am I goin' to do?" Clancy cuddled down beside her on the deep burgundy velvet sofa and propped his feet on the massive oak coffee table. She pushed a button on the remote and the TV came on.

"About what? Working at the company? Red's office staff will take you under their wings and smother you half to death. Those women have been with him since I've known him. Hell, they're probably the same women you used to visit with when you and your daddy came down here on Saturdays. The geologist and the lawyer are pretty new, but they're friendly. You'll like them. In a couple of weeks, you'll fit right in. Don't worry." She snuggled her body next to his and kissed him on the cheek. "Now, what do we intend to do about us?"

"Us?" he asked.

"Yep, us," she said "I'm in love with you, Clancy Morgan. And I don't intend to let some smooth-talking hussy take you away from me this time." She nibbled on his earlobe and he groaned.

"I intend to court you like a lady. I intend to take you everywhere I didn't take you all those years ago, and I fully intend to beg you until you say you'll marry me," Clancy said honestly.

"I hope so," she sighed. "Now can we just watch this movie and be still for a while? I want to feel you near me, but I don't want to make wild, passionate love—all this just plain wore me out. But I want to fall asleep in your arms and wake up to find you beside me, but before I do it, I want to hear you say—"

"I love you, Angel. I've loved you for ten years," Clancy kissed her on top of the forehead and knew another moment of blessed contentment.

"We might fight," she purred.

"We'll make up," he said.

"We might disagree. I'm obnoxious when I disagree," Angel said pertly.

"So am I, but for now, let's just think about today." Clancy pulled her even closer and leaned his head back on the velvet couch and shut his eyes. Way down deep in his soul he knew this was right, and he loved the feeling.

Fifteen

"Mornin', Angel," Patty greeted her with a big innocent smile.

"Call them all in," Angel said in the meanest voice she could muster. "Just us girls, in the conference room in three minutes, pronto."

The grin faded from Patty's face in an instant. She pushed the red button on the intercom sitting on her desk and said, "Angel's home, ladies. She says meet in three minutes in the conference room, and I think she means it. We're in trouble."

Angel looked down at the main street of Denison while she waited for her friends to assemble behind her. She wanted them to think she was so angry she didn't want to face them, but it was hard to keep a smile off her face. Especially when she thought about Red in his hospital bed trying to act more sick than he really was, and when she thought about waking up beside Clancy this morning. She'd opened her eyes half an hour before the alarm sounded, and she spent that time lying next to him, thinking about the future and what it would be like to watch Red and Tom both play with their grandchildren.

Patty cleared her throat and Angel turned around to find all five sitting in their places around the conference table. "I ought to shoot every one of you for the stunt you pulled, but for once your intuition was better than mine. I have to thank you." She smiled brightly.

Patty wiped her brow with the back of her hand in a dramatic gesture. Mindy sighed. Allie rolled her eyes to the ceiling, and Susan giggled.

"Want to tell us about it?" Bonnie smiled back and Angel figured that she'd been in charge of the whole set-up.

"Nope." Angel shook her head. "After what you did, not one of you deserves to hear the details. But Clancy and I intend to get on with the future and put the past behind us. This weekend he'll probably move from his old place in Oklahoma City, and I'm here where I belong. Trying to keep the bunch of you in line. Now, Susan, bring me up to date on what's going on in the front office. The rest of you have to meet with me at thirty-minute intervals . . ."

"Hey . . ." Bonnie stopped her midsentence. "We're your friends. We've shared evening from busted fingernails to divorces. We only did this to help you get over the sorry sucker who made you walk around here all down in the mouth."

"I'm over the past," Angel smiled at her friends. "I told you that." She suppressed a giggle.

Then she started to laugh. One minute everything was as quiet as a prelude to a funeral, the next minute Angel was wiping tears from her face and hiccuping. "You are all a bunch of devils," she said. "Clancy is moving in with me. We're goin' to make it this time! I've realized anything worth having is worth fightin' for, and no one is getting between me and Clancy Morgan again. Maybe I should have fought for him all those years ago, but then if I had, we wouldn't be where we are today. Clancy and I needed ten years to grow up enough to realize what we have . . . and I thank my bunch of honky-tonk devils for seeing that when I was blind.''

"Hot damn," Patty swore loudly. "Is there goin' to be a weddin'?"

"Maybe someday." Angel nodded.

"Someday . . ." Allie drew out the word and raised an eyebrow.

"Let's get back to business," Angel said. "And you should know that Red has hired a new man, who's pretty sharp. His name just happens to be Clancy Morgan and I don't think even *I* will be able to blink my pretty lashes and get him to give me a good deal," she told them.

"Well, isn't it a small world," Mindy said. "Angel, it might take a while for us to forgive that man, but we promise to give him a chance. Right, girls?" She grinned and disappeared out the side door to the hallway leading to her office.

"Nothing much has happened since you've been away," Susan said. "Except for Red's heart attack. Shook us all up. We reckoned he'd be around until eternity." She toyed with a lock of her short red hair. "Life sure don't offer any guarantees, does it, Angel? I think I'm goin' to tell Richie to set the date. Maybe a Thanksgiving wedding would be good. Bonnie will be married by then. I think I'll suggest we fly to Jamaica, for the holiday and tie the knot down there."

"If that's what you want, then go after it," Angel led the way from the conference room to her office and sat down behind her desk. "I'm hoping that Clancy and I will just wake up some morning and know that it's the day and find us a judge."

"I'm really happy for you," Susan said. "Guess he

turned out better than we expected. Can't punish him forever for a mistake he made ten years ago."

"Ain't that the truth." Angel opened a portfolio on her desk and reviewed Susan's proposition for a new advertising campaign. "Looks really good," she muttered, turning the pages. "Let me know when you're ready to spring it on the oil industry."

"Will do, and it's good to have you home. Gotta run. Never know what might come walkin' in the front door," Susan stood up and smoothed the wrinkles out of her emerald-green column dress.

Angel had barely gotten through her minimeetings with each of her friends when Patty buzzed to tell her Clancy was on the phone. "I've forgotten it all," he moaned when she picked up the remote phone and went to the window to watch the people on Main Street. "They're talking drillers and roughnecks and rigs and casings, and my mind is in a whirl. I knew the terminology at one time, but damn it all, it's gone now!"

"You'll learn. You're not that old, Clancy," she said seriously. "Remember, anything worth having is worth fighting for. Like Red told you last night, half of Texanna Red is yours right now. If you want to keep it, you'll learn."

"How can I learn this and court you, too? I can't think about business for thinking about you," he said.

"Then you better learn to control your thoughts a little better. From nine to five only think about Texanna Red, and from then on you belong to me," Angel laughed.

"Are we still going to the farm tonight? Do we have to go across that high bridge, or can we go up the highway and across?" he asked.

"Clancy, it's twice as far to go the highway, and it only takes thirty seconds to cross the bridge over into Hendrix. I'll drive," she said shortly. She couldn't imagine anyone being so afraid of heights. How in the world was he ever going to put on a hard hat and climb to the top of a rig for an inspection?

"Are we fighting?" he asked just as shortly.

"Who knows?" she said. "But we'll talk about it later. I've got a meeting with Margie this afternoon and I'd rather do battle with the Hendrix bridge any day than that old barracuda. You better hope Red is up and well by the time she knows you're a new person in the office. She'll eat you for lunch and lick her fingers afterward."

"You think I can't hold my own with her?" Clancy's voice held a challenging edge.

"Not if you don't learn the difference between a rig and a casing," she threw right back at him.

"I'll see you at five. And *I'll* drive over the Hendrix bridge. We'll take my Bronco," he said authoritatively.

"Anything you say, sweetheart. Have a good day," she said acidly.

Good grief, were they going to bicker like this every day? This was not good. Perhaps she and Clancy should live together before they really thought seriously about a permanent commitment, because Angel certainly didn't need this kind of conflict in her life every day.

She was still mulling the matter over in her mind when she arrived at the apartment that evening. Clancy's Bronco sat in the driveway beside her parking place. She opened the door and found his bags packed beside the door, but he was sleeping soundly on the couch. She sat down on the floor beside him and stared at him for ten minutes, trying to figure out what she should do. Would it be best to send him on his merry way? He might be her competitor forever, and then he wouldn't be her lover anymore.

That old familiar feeling tickled the inside of her mind and Angel knew without another thought what she was going to do. Clancy was going to face some difficult times as he learned a new business and had to face more responsibility than he'd ever faced before. She'd be there for him, and if they fought along the way, then they could damn well make up afterward, because she was committing herself for the long haul right now.

She leaned over and kissed him on the cheek. "Hey, sleepyhead, we've got to go see Red, and I called Hilda. Supper will be on the table at seven, so you'd better wake up and face the dreaded bridge."

"Shut up." He didn't open his eyes, but he did smile. "You know how afraid I am of heights. Always have been. Couldn't even dive off the dam because it looked like it was six miles to the bottom."

"I know." She kissed his eyelids and his cheeks, rough with a five o'clock beard. And then his mouth. "But you'll get over it."

They found Red sitting up in bed with a cordless phone and a yellow legal pad in front of him. Anna's jeans were creased perfectly and she'd visited the hairdresser that day. "Hey, how'd the first day go? Dennis, the geologist, said you were frustrated but determined." Red held up a hand. "By the way, I want the offshore drillers to start spending three weeks out and three weeks in. Give them more time at home with their families at a stretch."

"He's back to wheelin' and dealin'," Anna said

cheerfully. "I'm takin' him home and he'll be back at work by noon, but only for half a day this week. Doc says it'll be two weeks before he can go all day. You'll do fine, Clancy. In a while, you'll know as much about it as us old dogs. You younguns learn fast."

"Now, talk to me about you two." Red pushed the off button and set the phone down. "I want to know why neither of you ever mentioned the other's name in all these years."

"Wasn't any reason," Clancy said. "I didn't know Angel was in the oil business, and I figured she was off and married to someone else."

"I thought he and Melissa were married and living happily ever after, amen," Angel said. "And my intuition didn't tell me different."

Red chuckled. "Must be the only time it's failed you. I'd still pay you big bucks to sit behind a desk and tell me when that crazy feeling hits you. Clancy, if you don't take advantage of this girl's sixth sense, you're a lunatic."

"Yes, sir," Clancy saluted. "I shall take every known advantage of her, Red. And I'll be damned glad when you're back on the job to answer all my questions, because she's the competition and she's pretty close-mouthed when it comes to information I could use."

"Good for you." Red looked at Angel with pride. "Keep him on his toes and make him work for what he wants. In the business *and* in the bedroom."

"Red!" Angel blushed.

"Get on out of here." The older man waved them away. "I've got a decision or two to make and I don't have your instincts. I have to think," he told her. "Let me know when you decide to tie the knot. I've got a great honeymoon in mind. Hell, me and Anna just might go with you."

"No, we will not!" Anna exclaimed. "The doctor said no honeymoon activities for a while, you old lizard."

"See you." Angel kissed Red on the forehead. "But when and if Clancy and I decide to waste time and money on a honeymoon, we'll go alone."

"If you two are even thinking about a honeymoon, just remember that the wedding has to come first," Red said firmly. He tucked his chin in and studied her over the top of his gold-rimmed glasses.

"I know that." Her tone was as firm as his.

"Well, damn it all, Anna. She ain't softened up one bit with someone to love her, after all," Red grinned.

"See you at work tomorrow, Clancy." He waved as they left the room.

They left town in the Bronco, Clancy behind the wheel, his knuckles getting whiter as they got closer to the Hendrix bridge. His jaw was set in determination and he turned on the radio to distract himself, but he didn't talk to her. He would drive fifty extra miles a day not to have to look down at the Red River flowing under that rickety old bridge, but if she wanted to go this way, then by damn, this was the way they would go.

"Clancy, turn this car around and go the other way," Angel said when they were about a mile from the bridge. "Or else move over and let me drive."

"Hell, no!" he practically shouted. "I'm driving this way and I'm driving across that bridge."

"Have it your way." She clammed up and stared out

the side window. She couldn't fight his phobia for him, so he was going to have to overcome it or learn to let her drive. She sure wasn't going to fight this war every day.

His heart started doing double time when he saw the bridge ahead. Two kids riding bicycles were crossing, coming toward them, so he had to edge the Bronco off to the side and stop to let them across. He gripped the steering wheel as tightly he had the first time his father had let him drive at the age of eleven, and started across the bridge. He wanted to close his eyes, but knew better. Right in the middle, he stomped the brakes and sent up a silent prayer that the bridge wouldn't collapse and send the Bronco and both of them into the Red River. If it did, at least they'd go out of this life together.

"Come here," Clancy said hoarsely, and she moved across the bench seat to his side. "Sit by me and let me feel your warmth, Angel. I've been thinking ever since we left the hospital. I'm scared of this new change and I'm damned scared of this stupid bridge. But I can overcome anything with you beside me."

"That's right, Clancy . . . you can." Angel snuggled against him. "Now, let's get across this bridge. We've crossed worse, you know. In the past month, we've crossed a lot of bridges. I've met you in the middle of some of them, and you've had to meet me in the middle of some that were higher than this. We can make it together, honey. Let's go home."

"Before we do, I want to ask you right here on top of this hellacious bridge if you'll marry me, Angel. I still don't deserve you after what I did, but I'm hopelessly in love with you." He kissed her and forgot about where they were.

"Okay," she said. "Whenever and wherever you say. When you're ready, call the tune, and I'll dance to it. But darlin' there's a pickup waiting for us right now, so any more discussion has to wait until we get home."

He looked up to see a farmer grinning from ear to ear, waiting patiently in a beat-up, rusty red truck on the other side of the bridge.

"She said she'd marry me!" Clancy shouted to the farmer when they drove past, and the man gave him another big toothless smile and a thumbs-up sign.

Hilda opened the farmhouse door for them with a big smile on her face. She could tell at one glance that Angel had found happiness at last. Although this big, handsome man had done her wrong at one time, he could make up for it by spending the whole rest of his life taking care of her Miss Conrad. The housekeeper put a supper fit for royalty on the table, then declared she had to get home to her own family and couldn't possibly stay to help them eat.

"Just stack the dishes on the counter when you're finished. I'll put them in the dishwasher tomorrow morning, but I won't be here until after you leave for work. My great-granddaughter has a dance recital tomorrow and I promised her I would attend." Hilda hung her apron on the hook beside the stove. "And one more thing, young man," she pointed her finger at Clancy's nose and didn't smile or blink, "if you ever make Angel cry again, you'll have to deal with me. And when I finish, the buzzards get the leftovers. Now have a good supper."

"Whew!" Clancy exclaimed when Hilda was gone.

"Did I pass inspection at last? I can't tell by the way she talks."

"Yes, of course," Angel smiled. "Now will you hold me one more time and tell me what you said on that bridge? Now that you're not scared you're about to fall into the Red River. I think you proposed."

He dropped down on one knee and took her hand in his. "Will you marry me, Angel . . . next Friday night?"

"Yes, Clancy, I'll marry you, but why next Friday night?" she asked.

"You'll see." He stood up and gathered her into his arms for a kiss that sealed their promises and their hearts together forever and ever.

Epilogue

"What am I doing?" Angel looked in the mirror the very next Friday night. The same old girl she saw every morning looked back at her, but she didn't have any answers to the questions in Angel's heart. "Well, it's time," she said to her reflection. "Feels kind of crazy, but hey, I said whenever and wherever. If this is what Clancy wants, I'm willing to do it."

Angela got into her shiny Jaguar and drove down Main Street in Tishomingo. The city rolled up the sidewalks at five o'clock and only one red light worked after ten, even if it was Friday night. She passed a few cars full of kids out for a drive, but mostly the little town was quiet. She made a sharp right turn across the Pennington Creek bridge and carefully drove her car to the sandbar where a few people waited in folding chairs.

Red met her at the car. He wore his best western-cut suit with a carnation on the lapel, and his brand-new eelskin boots he'd just gotten from his bootmaker. "You're beautiful, and I'm glad for this honor." He took her arm.

Fiddle music began off to one side. Then she heard Mindy on the keyboard, playing a few soft chords. This was a surprise! Clancy had said there would be a few people and the girls, but that their wedding would be small, and now the band was set up to one side playing as Red led her down the aisle between the two rows of chairs.

"Who gives this woman to be married to this man?" the minister asked, but his voice didn't boom like it did in the church.

"Her friends and I do," Red said as he handed Angel's hand to Clancy.

Dillon continued. "We are gathered here because this is the time of night that Clancy first met Angel . . . and this is the time of night, I'm told, that they parted company exactly ten years ago this day. Clancy says this is what he should have done that night. And now we're doing something not everyone gets to do in their lifetime. We're getting to go back in time."

"Angel, I've got something to tell you," Clancy said loud and clear, remembering the words he'd spoken ten years ago. She was even more beautiful tonight, standing before him in a simple white cotton dress with white baby roses braided into a crown for her unruly hair.

"And I've got something to tell you, Clancy," Angel repeated the words she'd said and wondered what they were supposed to do next, since there weren't exactly alone. This time she couldn't tell him she was pregnant, because she wasn't . . . not yet.

"I'll go first," Clancy said, looking down into her beautiful green eyes. "I love you with my whole heart, Angel. It's been branded with your name for the past ten years and I want to stay with you forever, through this lifetime and eternity."

Her five friends brushed away tears of joy as Angel responded in an almost inaudible voice.

"Clancy, I took one look at you when we were still kindergarten and I wanted to stay with you forever. And now I will, through this lifetime and eternity, too."

The minister spoke again.

"Angela Conrad and Clancy Morgan have made their vows. These solemn promises are binding in the sight of God and these witnesses, and we come to the giving and receiving of rings," he said. And the otherwise traditional ceremony continued, up to and including a very untraditionally passionate kiss.

Later that night, in the privacy of their bedroom at the farmhouse, they ate the cheese and fruit left by Hilda, and tasted the sweetness of a bottle of Asti. Then Clancy undressed her slowly in the moonlight, wonder filling every fiber of his soul, that Angel was actually his wife. And then he carried her to the bed, where he gently laid her down.

"I love you, Mrs. Morgan, and I hope we have a dozen children," he whispered into her ear.

"I love you, too, Clancy. Now let's get started . . ."